Only The
Strong
Survive

Luxury Styles

ONLY THE STRONG SURVIVE
Copyright © 2020 by Luxury Styles

Cover and Interior design by August Pride, LLC.

ISBN: 978-1-950681-38-9

Ordering Information:

Quantity sales. Special discounts are available on quantity purchases by corporations, associations, and others. For details, contact the publisher at the address below.

ILLUMINATION PRESS
1100 Peachtree Street
Suite 250
Atlanta, GA 30309
InspirationalAuthors.com

Dedication

This book is dedicated to my brother, Theo

Brotherly Love

My Brother, My Friend

The Special Bond

What Fun We Had

The Time We Shared

Brother And Sister Forever

Acknowledgements

. . . .

First and foremost, I want to give God all the praise and glory for His favor and blessings. With God on my side, all things are possible.

I want to personally thank my wonderful family for being there every step of the way and for giving me the enormous support throughout my journey.

To all of my awesome friends – you know who you are. Thank you for the valuable advice, the respect, the tough love, and much more that has helped me succeed in life.

Special thanks to O.J. and R.K. who believed in me and guided me to start viewing things from a completely different perspective. Thinking and stepping outside of the box.

I especially want to thank Ms. May – the one who inspired me to follow my dreams. Dreams have no limits. Never give up on your dreams!

I would like to express my grateful gratitude and sincere appreciation to Benecia Ponder and everyone on the publishing team – it takes a village to write a book.

Table of Contents

. . . .

CHAPTER 1

Caught off Guard

· · · · · · · · · · · ·

"Where the hell do you think you are going?"

The booming voice shattered the quiet stillness around me and caused me to stumble on the narrow road. The lights from the car approaching me were blinding. In the darkness of the night, I could not clearly see the car or its driver, but I would recognize that loud, arrogant voice anywhere - Sergeant Cobra.

Damn! What does he want now? I am not in the mood for his shenanigans tonight.

Sergeant Cobra had already gotten on my nerves earlier. Ever since I transferred to this base a few months ago, he made it a top priority to single me out on a daily basis. He knew that I was a star athlete during my previous assignment, winning championships with the female basketball team and breaking distance and speed records with the track team. He would often make snide remarks and inappropriate comments about me and my appearance. Today, he yelled at me while we were standing in formation. After stepping on the boots I had so diligently shined, he bumped into me and said,

"The military is no place for women like you."

After he dismissed us, I contemplated his behavior for only a few moments before putting him out of my mind. I didn't let him ruin my day and I am not about to let him ruin my night.

Keeping my eyes on the road ahead, I picked up my pace, hoping if I ignored him, he would just go away.

No such luck.

Sergeant Cobra pulled his car to a stop beside me, and I instantly regretted telling Liberty I would meet her at the club instead of riding with her.

Liberty and I met a few years ago while stationed at my previous base. She was funny and easy to talk to, so when we were transferred to this base at the same time, Liberty and I became very good friends. She knew I needed to let off some steam after a grueling week of dealing with Sergeant Cobra and suggested we go to the NCO club for drinks and dancing. Liberty was in a different company so she didn't have to deal directly with Sergeant Cobra's tirades, but she was very familiar with his reputation for being tough on women, especially the strong ones who didn't cower to his tyranny.

I was just getting out of the shower when she stopped by my room half an hour ago so we could ride over to the club together. It wouldn't take long for me to get ready; I wasn't dressing up or anything. Liberty had on a silky blouse, a tight skirt and heels; her face was fully made up and she had big hoops sparkling on her ears. It probably had taken her more than an hour to get ready.

I, on the other hand, was not so high maintenance. It would take me less than ten minutes to put on my white t-shirt, khaki cargo pants, and brown Timberland boots, no makeup or accessories necessary. Nevertheless, I told Liberty to go on. I didn't want her playing dress up with me. I told her I would see her in a few minutes at the club.

It's only a ten-minute walk from the barracks to the club. I'll be fine, I'd said.

Now I wished I would have told her to wait.

When I didn't stop to answer him, Sergeant Cobra jumped out of his car and started yelling at me.

"Where the hell are you going? You shouldn't even be out here. Where is your off-duty pass, Private?"

Deciding to end this once and for all, I pulled out my pass. I didn't speak a word as I held it up for him to see.

Sergeant Cobra ripped the card from my hand. With surprise, I watched as he began tearing it to pieces right in front of my face.

"I guess you don't have a pass after all, huh?" he snarled, as he continued to shred the paper.

I watched the pieces flutter to the ground like confetti and felt the white heat of anger rising up inside of me.

Ever since I'd arrived at this base, this man had been deliberately causing problems for me.

He constantly berated me and found every possible way to make my life a living hell.

Being in the military for almost four years, I knew how hard it was for women. Although they considered us to be weaker and unable to do much, the commanding officers were twice as hard on us.

I tried my best not to think about how much I hated this man. However, despite my best efforts, I was obsessed by the thought of how good it would feel to rip every hair out of his head, one by one. Before I could act on my thoughts, I turned around and began walking back to the barracks. The night was over even before it began.

I was halfway between the barracks and the club. In five minutes, I would be back in my room. Hopefully, the walk would cool me off and I could get some sleep. I definitely was not in the mood to party anymore.

I took only a few steps before Sergeant Cobra yelled again.

"Get in the car!" he bellowed.

It took a second for me to process his words.

He wanted me to get into his car? No, thank you. There was no way in hell I would get into a car with him. I would walk a million miles before I did that.

I continued to walk towards the barracks in silence, pretending I did not hear his command. Sergeant Cobra caught up to me. He grabbed my arm and spun me around.

"I said, get in the car. Now! I am taking you back to the barracks," he ordered.

He was inches in front of my face, and I could smell the liquor oozing from his pores.

Taking a deep breath, I weighed my options. I observed the scene around me. Other than the lights from Sergeant Cobra's car, the night was pitch black. No other cars were passing on this two-lane road. It was Friday night and everyone in this small military town was either already at the club or had headed into the next town to party. It was just the two of us on this dark isolated road.

I wasn't afraid though.

This guy was just a big bully. He barked loudly, but he was weak.

Echoing the words I had spoken to Liberty earlier, I finally broke my silence, "It's only a short walk. I'll be fine, sir."

Forcing myself to remain poised and in control, I kept my voice steady. Sergeant Cobra looked coiled and ready to strike.

My calm demeanor only seemed to enrage him even more. He was used to making the females in his company cry with his abusive behavior, but I never did. I didn't let him get to me. Men like this were pathetic and I refused to let him get under my skin.

I am Strong.

He might outrank me in position, but I was far superior in intellect and class. I would not stoop to his level. I was determined to show him the respect his position demanded, even though he did not deserve it.

I took a few steps back and tried to continue my walk to the barracks. Sergeant Cobra quickly closed the gap. He grabbed my arm and twisted hard.

"I am not going to tell you again. Get in the car. I am taking you back to the barracks."

A look into his cold, dark eyes sent a chilly shiver down my spine. Sudden fear replaced my anger and annoyance.

Sergeant Cobra outweighed me by at least a hundred pounds. He towered more than half a foot over me. The vice grip he had on my arm tightened and I squirmed.

I looked around to see if there was any way of escaping this situation. I could see the outline of the barracks in the distance. It wasn't that far away. I was a track star, after all. Outrunning him would be easy. I could get to the barracks before he could even get back to his car. But what would I do then? I would not be able to avoid him for long. Running from him now would only make things worse later.

I decided to play it cool. The ride would be less than three minutes and I could handle anything for three minutes, right?

I walked over to the passenger's side of Sergeant Cobra's car. Pulling the back door open, I slid in. I would obey his request to take me back to the barracks, but there was no way I was going to sit in the front seat next to him.

As I moved into the car, the glowing red numbers on the dashboard clock caught my attention—12:17.

I should have been on my second drink by now. I really need at least a few shots after this.

I started to close the door, but it was blocked. I pulled harder, then looked up.

Instead of going to the driver's side, Sergeant Cobra had followed me to the passenger's side. As I was trying to close the door, he was holding it open.

I looked at him in confusion. *What the hell?*

Before I could say a word, he pushed me back on the seat. Dazed, I wheezed for air as his forearm crushed my windpipe. He paralyzed me with his elbow in my throat as he pulled down my loose-fitting cargo pants with his other hand. I struggled against him, but with his arm cutting off my air supply, I was suffocating. Every move I made only deepened the pressure.

The look in his eyes stopped me cold.

7

I have never seen a look like that. He was crazed. His eyes were glazed over with a gleam that looked more animalistic than human. Terror coursed through me. I was being attacked by a vicious beast.

Sergeant Cobra seemed to have the strength of a six-hundred-pound grizzly bear as he held me down. When he finally got my pants down, he ripped my panties and raped me.

I was in shock. Pain radiated from my neck where he choked me all the way down to the intimate places where he had violated me.

When he was finished, he released his hold on my throat. I slowly turned my head, gasping for air. As I turned my head from side to side, the glowing red numbers on the dashboard once again caught my attention—12:20.

As I stared at the glowing red numbers, I realized only three minutes had passed.

You can handle anything for three minutes, huh? a sarcastic voice in my head taunted me.

Apparently, the Universe was putting that theory to the test. In three minutes, something I had never imagined would happen had turned my world upside down.

The cracked leather of the seat dug into my skin and I could feel the weight of Sergeant Cobra's body still hovering over me.

My mind started to spin, trying to come to grips with my current predicament.

How had this happened? Why would he do something like this?

I knew Sergeant Cobra was menacing, but I never in a million years thought he was capable of doing something like this.

"If you tell anyone about this, I will kill you," Sergeant Cobra growled.

His cruel voice snapped me back to my senses. I shook my head to clear my thoughts.

The paralyzing shock quickly morphed into rage. Raising my booted foot I aimed at the vile part of him that had traumatized me. I hit my target with such a force that he fell back out of the car.

While he writhed on the ground clutching himself, I pulled up my pants and did what I should have done before—I ran.

Each step I took intensified my pain. But the pain radiating through my body was no match for the pain that permeated my soul.

I had to keep running though. I could not slow down or stop. I did not hear Sergeant Cobra behind me, but that did not mean anything. At any moment he could pop up to torment me again.

I ran like my life depended on it. And it did. All I could hear was Sergeant Cobra's voice ringing in my ears,

"If you tell anyone about this, I will kill you."

How could I tell anyone? Who would even believe me?

It was just the two of us on the road. It would be my word against his. A Private versus a Senior Sergeant. Who would believe me over him?

I was grateful to reach the barracks without being caught. As with the road, the barracks were deserted. I was grateful for that, too. I did not want to risk anyone seeing me like this. I did not want to take the chance of blurting out what happened.

"If you tell anyone about this, I will kill you."

I could not even tell Liberty. She was a feisty firecracker with a quick temper. Just that day she had gotten into a fight with another female who had gotten in her face. She was not the type to let things go without retaliation. If I told her, she would definitely go after Sergeant Cobra. It would be a huge mess.

I walked to my room and laid on my bed. I felt soiled but did not have the energy to stand any longer.

I did not bother getting under the covers. I just curled up in a ball with my clothes and shoes still on. My mother had given me the soft gray comforter and I usually felt warm and safe when it covered me. But I could not be comforted now.

In three minutes, my life had changed forever. Nothing will ever be the same. I will never be able to trust anyone ever again. I knew Sergeant Cobra was mean, but I didn't think he was savage. He was like a wild, feral animal. How could a person who vowed to protect and serve do something like this? He was supposed to protect me from harm's way.

Was it me?

Could I have done something to provoke him?

Should I have just gotten in the car when he asked the first time?

Why didn't I ride to the club with Liberty? I could have avoided this whole thing.

As I rocked myself back and forth, trying to soothe my erratic emotions, I felt my body go numb. I do not know how long it was before I drifted off to sleep. One moment my mind was racing with anxiety and the next...

Was that a dog barking?

Who has a dog in the barracks?

I jolted up on the bed; that dream was weird. Why was I dreaming about barking dogs?

I rubbed my eyes and realized I was not dreaming. There was a dog barking in the barracks.

Before I could fully process this odd occurrence, the door to my room slammed open and Sergeant Cobra's voice rang out,

"Private Strong, get up now!"

CHAPTER 2
Falsely Accused
· · · · · · · · · · · ·

I blinked my eyes rapidly, trying to get them to adjust to the sudden change from total darkness to bright light. As the room came into focus, I saw Sergeant Cobra standing in the doorway. Behind him were two military police officers and a K-9 dog barking furiously. Were these officers here to question me about what happened tonight? Had someone seen what Sergeant Cobra did to me? Did they report it to the Military Police? Were these officers here to confirm with me? Were they about to arrest him?

Sergeant Cobra had an angry sneer on his face and a dangerous glint in his eyes. He had changed clothes since I saw him last. Had it been an hour ago? Two hours ago? The lights were turned off, I couldn't see the clock in my room; I had no idea how much time had passed since I escaped his attack.

I felt a chill run down my spine as Sergeant Cobra pierced me with his intense gaze. His next words completely froze me.

"Private First Class Strong, you are a dangerous person and you will not be sleeping in the barracks tonight."

Sergeant Cobra's voice seemed to be too big for the small room. I fought the urge to cover my ears because I needed to hear the words coming out of this man's mouth. I could not possibly be hearing him clearly.

Did he just say I was a dangerous person?

Maybe I was still dreaming. Was this a dream within a dream?

Was this man really saying that I was dangerous?

Me?

He was the dangerous one. He was the one who assaulted me. My body was still in pain from his abuse. *How could he say that I was dangerous?*

I shook my head in an attempt to make some sense of this bewildering situation. Apparently, I had entered a twilight zone where everything was backwards.

"Dangerous? *I'm* dangerous?" I asked in confusion.

My voice sounded tiny and distant as if I was hearing it from far away.

"How am I dangerous?" I asked.

I looked behind Sergeant Cobra to get the attention of the military police officers. They were here to help me, right? Maybe they could help me navigate this alternate universe. None of this was making any sense.

I was the one who had been attacked. I was the one who had been violated.

I am not dangerous, far from dangerous.

He is dangerous.

Sergeant Cobra advanced toward me, blocking my line of sight to the officers. His voice boomed out as he approached until he was standing right in front of my bed.

"You heard me! You are dangerous. You will not be allowed to stay in the barracks tonight," he spat out.

From my position on the bed, Sergeant Cobra's crotch was right in front of my face. Flashbacks of his aggressive violence towards me raced through my mind. Was he about to attack me again? In front of these officers? Why did they just stand there and let him get so close and speak to me that way?

I shrank back and tried to put some distance between my face and his crotch. But there was only so far I could go. I backed up on my tiny twin bed until my back hit the concrete wall.

He was still too close to me.

I put my hands up to stop him. I could not stand him being this close to me, especially after what he had done.

All of my senses were on high alert and my fight or flight response was triggered. There was nowhere to run in this tiny room so my only option was to fight.

I balled my hands into fists and stiffened my body preparing to defend myself. He was not going to force himself on me again.

"No!" I shouted.

I started to tell him that I was not dangerous and that I was not going to let him bully me any longer.

The first word was barely out of my mouth before I found myself on the cold, hard floor. In a split second, the military officers who were standing behind Sergeant Cobra charged forward. They grabbed me from the bed and slammed me on the floor. I felt a knee in the center of my back. Excruciating pain radiated throughout my already sore body.

What was going on?

I thought they were here to help me. Why were they holding me down?

The K-9 dog's bark grew louder and more furious. I felt the cold metal of handcuffs being forced around my wrists.

"I didn't do anything," I pleaded. "It was him. He's the one…"

My words were drowned out by the dog's barking and Sergeant Cobra's rancid voice.

"Shut up! We are taking you into custody." Sergeant Cobra said loudly, drowning out my protests.

Wake up! I shouted silently to myself. You must wake up from this crazy nightmare!

The military police officers pulled me to my feet and dragged me out of my room with Sergeant Cobra following close behind. From the looks of things, it had to be after two o'clock in the morning. I could tell because the NCO club closed at two and the club goers were just starting to trickle back into the barracks. Some of them looked on in shock as I was hauled through the barracks. I could only imagine how I must look in their half-drunk eyes.

I still wore the same white t-shirt, cargo pants, and boots I had on when Sergeant Cobra assaulted me. My once pristine and starch pressed shirt was filthy and crumpled. My pants were torn, my boots were scuffed and streaked with mud from my run back to the barracks, and my hair, which had once been secured in a neat bun, was now a matted mess.

"Leave her alone. Let her go," I heard someone yell as we passed by.

The officers did not say a single word as we continued out of the building.

The night air felt cool. For some reason the only thought that passed through my mind was, *I'm so glad I didn't take my clothes and shoes off before going to bed.*

Then it struck me. I was still wearing the clothes I was wearing when Sergeant Cobra attacked me. All of a sudden, I felt filthy. My skin crawled with the memories of Sergeant Cobra on top of me.

His words ricocheted in my mind, "If you tell anyone about this, I will kill you."

Was this his way of ensuring that I would not talk to anyone?

As the police officers shoved me into the back of their car, I realized I had no idea where they were taking me. I could see the questioning stares of my barracks-mates. They were wondering what I had done. I had no answers for them because I was wondering the same thing.

What had I done to deserve this kind of treatment?

Nothing.

Deep inside me I knew that I had not done anything to deserve this. I was being treated like a criminal, but I had done nothing wrong. I comforted myself with the knowledge that I was completely innocent. Whatever lies Sergeant Cobra told to have me handcuffed and thrown into the back of a police car would not last. I would tell the truth and his lies would be exposed.

I encouraged myself with these thoughts as we rode through the base. Despite the turmoil going on with me, everyone else on base seemed to be sleeping peacefully.

The car came to a stop in front of the Stockade Confinement Facility. This was where military personnel go to jail.

They were taking me to jail?!

The shock of the situation instantly wore off and transformed into panic. I did not belong here. I am not a criminal.

"What are we doing here?" I asked

The police officers ignored me. So I asked again,

"What are we doing here? Why have you brought me here? I have not done anything wrong."

Still, they said nothing. After a few moments, I heard a car pull up next to us. I turned to see Sergeant Cobra. The look in his eyes was pure evil.

The officers dragged me out of the car and led me into the building.

I was placed in a chair in front of a worn desk that looked as battered as I felt. The nameplate on the desk told me it belonged to the Clerk. The woman at the desk looked at me dismissively.

"Do you know why you are here?" she asked.

"No, I don't know why I am here," I said. "I have not done anything wrong."

"You don't think fighting and stabbing a person is wrong?"

"What? I have no idea what you are talking about. Fighting? Stabbing? I don't even have a knife."

They think I was in a fight and I stabbed someone? They must have me mistaken for someone else. All I need to do is tell her that I am not who they think I am. That will straighten this whole thing out. And, while I am here, I will tell them what Sergeant Cobra did. I was going to keep quiet, but this just added insult to injury. He knew I had not been in any fight tonight and he still let this happen.

"Ma'am…" I started to explain, "You have me mistaken for

someone else. I was not in a fight tonight. I did not stab anyone. I do not have a knife. I am not the person you are looking for."

"Tell it to the Captain," she said. "I am just here to process you. You can tell your lies to her. Maybe she will believe you."

Lies?

Lies!

I was not the one telling lies.

"When will I be able to talk to the Captain?" I asked.

Apparently, this woman was not going to help me.

The Clerk slid a piece of paper and a pen in front of me.

"What is this for?" I asked.

"Just sign it." she said without even looking at me.

I did my best to read the words, but I could barely think straight let alone concentrate enough to read. I could tell it was a form of some kind, but it didn't look like any military paperwork I had ever seen.

The Clerk had written my name and rank on a line at the top of the form. Under my name she had written some numbers and letters. The rest of the form had more words but for some reason my brain would not focus enough for me to comprehend them.

"Just sign the paper," the Clerk commanded again. "The sooner you sign, the sooner you will be able to speak to the Captain."

Too tired to question her further, I picked up the pen and signed the form next to the big "X" at the bottom.

"Now can I speak with the Captain?" I asked as I slid the form back to the Clerk.

"She will question you as soon as I am finished with the processing."

"Can you at least tell me where this fight supposedly happened? And who was stabbed?"

The Clerk looked at me and rolled her eyes.

"The fight happened at the NCO Club at around midnight. The person stabbed was a military female," she said impatiently as if this was information I already knew.

"At the NCO Club? It couldn't have been me," I protested. "I didn't even make it to the club. I was stopped before I could get there."

I was about to tell the Clerk just what—or should I say who— stopped me when the Captain walked into the room.

I had seen this woman before around the base. The rumor was that she and Sergeant Cobra were having an affair.

As the Captain approached me, I could see Sergeant Cobra standing in the doorway of the office she had just exited

"Private Strong, come with me."

The tone of her voice was gruff and commanding. The look in her eyes was dark and ominous.

I rose from the chair with apprehension. The Captain ushered me into her office past Sergeant Cobra. She gave him a slight nod and smile as she closed the door.

The Captain's office was slightly larger than my room in the barracks. A small wood desk sat on one side of the room and a cracked leather chair was behind the desk. Two metal folding chairs had been placed in front of the desk.

"Sit," she said, pointing to one of the metal chairs as she took her seat behind the desk.

"Sergeant Cobra has informed me of your activities tonight. I must say, I have seen you around the base and I would not have thought you were the fighting type. But apparently, you have a combative and aggressive nature that Sergeant Cobra has repri- manded you for on many occasions."

I was stunned. Not only was I being accused of fighting and stabbing someone, but I was also being accused of being combat- ive and aggressive?

I could not let this go on any further.

"Captain, I did not do any of the things I am being accused of. I did not get into a fight tonight. I did not stab anyone. I am not combative or aggressive."

"Really?" she asked as she read a piece of paper on her desk. "The report from the officers who brought you in tonight says that you tried to attack Sergeant Cobra."

"What? I did not attack him. He attacked me!" I shouted.

"Calm down, Private!" the Captain said sternly. "I can tell by your attitude right now that you are exactly as he said you are."

"With all due respect, Captain, you would be frustrated and angry too if you were being accused of something you did not do."

"Well, we will see about that. We will do a full investigation of the incident. In the interim, you will be held here."

The room seemed to be closing in on me as the gravity of the situation started to sink in,

"Captain, I did not do anything wrong. Sergeant Cobra is making this up. He is setting me up. It is all because he…"

"Enough!" she yelled, cutting me off in mid-sentence. "I do not want to hear another word from you."

"B-B-But…" I stammered.

"I said not one more word!"

The Captain rose from her chair. She walked around the desk and grabbed my arm. Opening the door to her office, she called out to the two officers who had brought me in.

"Take her to lock up," she told them.

Tears streamed down my face as one of the officers pushed me in the direction of a long hallway. I knew it would do no good to argue or fight. I walked down the hallway in silence with one officer on each side of me.

At the end of the hallway, there was a heavy metal door. One of the officers pushed the door open and the other one pushed me forward. Before crossing the threshold, I looked back towards the Captain's office. I saw Sergeant Cobra standing next to the Captain. They were huddled together talking. He seemed to feel my eyes on him and he looked up. As his eyes met mine, he winked.

CHAPTER 3
Locked Up

· · · · · · · · · · · ·

I was locked in a cell.

It was a tiny space with concrete walls and floors. Two sets of bunk beds faced each other with a narrow path in between. There was a metal toilet with no lid in the corner and a peephole sized window above it.

I looked around the cell in shock.

I did not belong here.

I didn't know how long I would be locked up, but surely it wouldn't be that long. All they had to do was a little bit of investigation to find out that I was not at the club last night and that I did not stab anyone.

I thought about the movies and wondered if I would get a phone call or be given an attorney.

My only consolation at the moment was that I had the small space to myself. I did not even want to imagine having to use that toilet in front of other people.

I laid down on one of the bottom bunks and tried to relax, but it was hard to get comfortable. The pillow was as flat as a pancake, the blanket was scratchy, and the mattress was lumpy. I tried to take in a deep breath to calm my nerves, but the smells that assaulted my nostrils made me gag.

My exhaustion finally took over and I drifted off to sleep. I am not sure how long it was before I was awakened by a clanking on the cell bars. There was an officer there holding a metal tray of food. From the sliver of light coming in from the window, I could tell it was morning.

The officer slid the tray through a slot in the cell bars and walked away. Just the thought of food had my stomach rumbling. I was starving.

I grabbed the tray and scanned the contents. It looked like the food we were normally served in the chow hall so I guessed it was okay to eat. Whatever it was, I was too hungry to be picky. I gobbled up the food in record time. I don't even think I tasted it.

I spent the next two days in complete isolation. Other than the officer who brought my food, I had no human interaction. Every time the officer dropped off and picked up the food tray, I asked him to tell me what was happening. He didn't say a word. He barely even looked my way.

"I am innocent!" I shouted after him when he brought me lunch on the third day.

When he came back to pick up the lunch tray, I said, "I did not stab anyone. I was the one who was attacked. Ask Sergeant Cobra."

Once again, he silently walked away.

After dinner on my fourth day of confinement, two girls were brought into my cell. I wondered what they had done to get locked up. They seemed pretty normal to me dressed in fatigues and boots. After being alone for so long, it was good to see other people. Even if we were locked up together. I gave a small smile and said,

"Hey, I'm Strong."

One of the girls looked at me and nodded. The other didn't say a thing or even look in my direction.

I tried to start a conversation, but neither of the women said a word.

Since dinner had already been served, there was nothing else to do for the evening. Not wanting to prolong the awkward silence any longer, I laid down on my bunk and went to sleep.

BAM!

In the middle of the night I felt a hit to the back of my head. One of the women pulled me off my bunk while the other one kicked me in the chest. I tried to scream for help but the woman who pulled me from my bunk hit me in the face so hard I almost blacked out.

After kicking me several more times, one of the women said, "You need to learn to keep your mouth shut."

I didn't know what she was talking about. Were they attacking me because I tried to start a conversation with them?

Then the other woman said, "Serge said you have been talking too much and he sent us to make sure you keep quiet."

Serge?

Did she mean Sergeant Cobra?

He sent them?

I closed my eyes and vowed that if I made it through this, I would never say anything about Sergeant Cobra ever again.

I must have blacked out because I woke up curled in a ball on the floor. I heard the sound of the food tray being slid into the food slot. The light from the window was shining on my face.

I opened my eyes and looked around the cell expecting to see the hard faces of the women who attacked me in the middle of the night, but they were not there.

If I did not have the sore ribs to prove they had been there, I would have thought it was all a bad dream.

CHAPTER 4
Secrecy

· · · · · · · · · · · ·

After seven long days of being tormented and traumatized in the Stockade Confinement Facility, I was finally released. The investigators spoke with the stabbing victim and she told them I was not the one who assaulted her. I cannot understand why it took them so long to talk to the victim, but I knew Sergeant Cobra somehow had something to do with it. The entire situation was a set up; it was his way of keeping me quiet about what he had done to me.

I decided that I was indeed going to keep quiet. If he could arrange for me to be falsely imprisoned and then orchestrate the brutal torture I experienced over the last week, I knew he would do anything to guarantee my silence. I would not put it past him to follow through with his threat to kill me. And, knowing how devious he was, he would surely make my death look like an accident or suicide.

Yes, I would keep my mouth shut, stay to myself, and avoid Sergeant Cobra as much as I could.

I walked out of the stockade and breathed in the fresh air. It was good to see the sky again after being surrounded by concrete. I looked around, not quite sure what to do. After telling me I was free to go, nothing else was said.

No apologies. No explanations. No offers of help. I was simply released and shown the door.

On my walk from the stockade to the barracks, I avoided eye contact with everyone I passed. I couldn't look at them. I did not want them to see the hurt and shame in my eyes.

The walk back to the barracks took about thirty minutes but I was glad that I was no longer restricted. My body still ached from the beatings.

The first thing I did when I arrived at my room was to strip off the clothes I'd been wearing for the past week. I wanted to burn them. They smelled like sweat and shame. They reminded me of the torture I had endured. They were a symbol of my destroyed innocence and loss of faith in humanity.

I stood in the shower for ten minutes, just allowing the warm water to wash over me. Then, I felt the first tear fall. I had not cried the entire time I was locked up, but now the dam broke. The water released the anguish I had been holding on to. The tears began to fall faster and soon I was sobbing. The sobs wracked my body and I could not control them. I am not sure how long I stood in the shower crying, but by the time the tears dried up the water was ice cold.

Feeling drained and defeated, I left the shower and returned to my room. I put on fresh clothes and crawled into bed. Flashbacks of the last time I was in this room flooded my mind. Sergeant Cobra bursting in…the MPs slamming me to the floor…the dog barking...it all came rushing back and the tears flowed again. I cried and rocked myself back and forth.

Why God? Why?

I continued to cry and rock until I fell asleep. When I woke up, I felt exhausted. I wasn't sure how long I was asleep, but it was not enough.

The day after I was released from lock up, I was notified that I was being transferred to another military base to carry out the rest of my military service. Three weeks later, I was on a plane traveling to a new base on the other side of the country.

CHAPTER 5

Deep In My Feelings

· · · · · · · · · · · ·

Something was wrong.

My transfer to the new base was uneventful, and my commanding officers were Mary Poppins compared to Sergeant Cobra. Yet, I could not settle into my new surroundings. From the moment I arrived at the new base, I struggled just to get out of bed every morning.

I was severely fatigued and the slightest activity totally exhausted my energy. I had body aches and some nausea. It felt as if I had the flu. That wasn't like me. Other than being, what my family called "skinny as a pole," I was always a healthy person.

When my symptoms did not get any better after several weeks, I went to the doctor's office to see what was wrong with me. The nurse took my vital signs, ran a variety of tests, and did lab work. It seemed to take forever to get the results back, which caused me to get very anxious. I did not think it should take so long for them to run a few tests. I sat in the cold exam room for more than thirty minutes and finally, I could not sit any longer. I started to walk around the room to calm my nerves. As I was pacing back and forth, the nurse came into my exam room. She told me to relax and to have a seat.

She had a huge smile on her face and looked at me with an excited gleam in her eyes. Obviously, whatever she had to tell me was good news. I started to relax and my breathing returned to normal, until she spoke...

"You are pregnant!" she enthusiastically exclaimed; her smile still wide.

I instantly threw my hands up in the air and screamed out loud, "Oh My Gosh!"

The nurse grimaced and her smile turned into a confused stare. She shook her head, trying to understand my severe reaction to what she apparently thought would be exciting news.

It was not good news for me. It was the worst news I could ever receive. If she would have told me I had a deadly virus or cancer, I probably would have responded much better than I did to finding out that I was pregnant.

I started pacing around the room again. My breathing became shallow and my mind started racing.

This could not be happening to me.

They must have switched my tests with someone else's.

All I have to do is get them to retake the tests.

They made a mistake.

This is a mistake.

As my mind raced, I began to shout out,

"NO!"

I just kept repeating the word over and over again as I continued to pace the room like an animal trapped in a cage.

The nurse left the room for a moment...maybe two or three... I am really not sure how long she was gone because all I could focus on was the devastating news she had given me. When she came back, she tried to get me to calm down. She spoke in slow, soothing tones as she told me there was nothing to worry about. She said everything would be okay. She would help me to get through this.

When the nurse finally calmed my hollering butt down, she gave me all kinds of motherhood pamphlets. As she tried to hand me the huge stack of papers, I refused to take them.

"I need to weigh my options," I said, stepping back so the papers would not even touch me.

"Options?" she asked gently. "Sweetheart, you do not have any options other than to have this baby. You are too far along to do anything else."

"Wait...what? Too far along? I can't be that far along." I said in confusion.

Then it hit me and I almost passed out. I grabbed onto the examination table to keep myself from hitting the floor.

The nurse confirmed my horrible suspicion when she said, "Darling, you are too far along in your pregnancy."

Immediately, Sergeant Cobra's menacing face leering over me in the back seat of his car flashed in my mind.

No! This could not be. I thought I had put that behind me and here it is again.

Suddenly, the room felt incredibly small. I could feel the walls closing in on me. I had to get out of there.

I jetted out of the doctor's office, and all I could hear was the nurse calling my name to come back. If that nurse only knew what I knew.

I lost my everlasting mind that day. I thought I went to hell and back. I was pregnant by Sergeant Cobra. I don't even know him, not even his first name, or anything else about him—other than the fact that he was the most despicable, hateful, and evil man I had ever known.

How would I explain to my child who their father is?

I went home and cried myself to sleep. I didn't know what to do. I could not tell my family about my pregnancy or about my assault because I did not know if they would have believed me or not. And, if they did believe me, that could be even worse. My brothers were always overprotective when it came to me – their baby sister, and I know they would do bodily harm or something even more awful to Sergeant Cobra if they would have found out the true story.

But I had to tell someone. I could not keep this bottled up inside. It would tear me apart.

The next day, I called my best friend, Vegas. I sadly told her the whole story—the assault, my false imprisonment, my pregnancy. I told her everything without holding any details back because I knew she was the only one that I could tell without receiving any judgment.

Vegas and I grew up together in Buffalo and we always had each other's backs through thick and thin. Trust me; I kept Vegas out of trouble or took the blame for her many times.

Vegas was very smart; she took the GED exam at the age of sixteen and passed the test with flying colors. Me, I have the three senses – Book Sense, Common Sense, and Street Sense – the Mastermind. We both were too darn smart for our own britches. The school teachers did not know what to do with us.

Vegas and I were like sisters, we had a lot in common, and we both came from a big family with a lot of siblings. The only difference between Vegas and me is that Vegas was born to a rich family.

Vegas was happily married with a little girl and she and her family had relocated to Manhattan. Despite the distance between her home and my new base, Vegas was right by my side when I gave birth to my baby boy. It wasn't a happy time; it was a sad occasion. I didn't want to see my baby when he was born due to the fact that he reminded me of the assault that took place. I just was so done with everything in my world. I didn't know how to handle this situation. I was giving my baby up for adoption, to strangers. This doesn't feel right. Vegas was feeling my pain.

The room was so quiet and suddenly Vegas said,

"I have an idea. Why don't you let me raise the baby? It would just be our little secret, no one has to know nothing, and we will just keep this on the down low."

You know what they say, "What goes on in Vegas, stays in Vegas."

I decided to name my baby son Empower. I held him in the palm of my hand and I told him that he has a strong name like his mother and that he is going to be somebody special one day.

Empower kicked his little feet and looked at me with his eyes wide open as if he knew what I was talking about.

After Empower and I were released from the hospital, I returned to my home on the military base and Vegas took Empower back to Manhattan with her. She promised to take great care of him, just as if he was her own. I knew I could trust Vegas to do just that.

The weeks that followed were lonely. I did not have any friends to turn to. I hadn't told my family about anything that was happening, so I could not reach out to them. As I struggled to deal with my confusing emotions, I wished I could talk to my mommy.

My mother was a single mother who raised seven kids by herself. When I was growing up, my mother was considered the neighborhood mother. Everyone in the community loved her and she made sure that no one went unfed. Everyone turned to her for advice when they were in trouble.

I nervously picked up the telephone and I called my mother. She was so happy to hear from me – her precious military daughter. She told me that she had just finished baking a birthday cake for my baby brother; he just turned eighteen years old.

A mother knows when something is wrong. I guess she heard the sorrow in my voice and she asked me,

"Is everything alright with you?"

"I'm f-f-fine," I managed to get out before breaking down in tears.

"Oh baby, what's wrong?" my mother asked.

"Mommy, my whole life is a mess," I cried.

My mother allowed me to cry for a few moments. Then she said,

"Tell me what's going on."

"I don't know what to do. Everything in my life is all screwed up." I told her.

My mother soothed me with her calm voice, "There's not anything that bad where we can't fix it."

I knew my mother meant exactly what she said. She was a resourceful woman and always seemed to know what to do. My mother assured me that whatever was going on, we would find a resolution. She told me that she and the rest of my family would be right by my side.

I planned a visit to go home in two weeks. I promised my mother I would tell her everything at that time. By the time our conversation ended, my spirits were lifted and I felt hope for the first time since I found out I was pregnant.

I went to work the next day with a big smile on my face. The others who worked in the office with me were surprised and commented on my positive mood. Since the time I had arrived on the base, they had never seen me smile.

When the telephone on my desk rang, I answered with a cheery, "Hello."

The woman on the other end of the line was from the communications office with an urgent message from my sister, Pyramid. The message was very brief. The only thing the woman said was, "You have a family emergency. You need to call home immediately."

As I dialed my sister's number, chills of dread ran through my body. My mind raced with various scenarios, all of which were devastating.

Pyramid answered the phone crying hysterically.

"What happened?" I asked her, not sure if I really wanted to know.

"It's M-M-Mommy…" she stammered.

"What happened? I just talked to her yesterday." I said.

The line was silent for a few moments. I could hear Pyramid's sobbing on the other end and I could tell she was trying to gather herself enough to speak.

"Mother died unexpectedly."

"Nooooooo!"

I dropped the phone and then punched the wall next to me. Without saying another word to Pyramid, I ran out of the building. I made it to a bench a few yards away and collapsed.

No…not my Mommy!

How could this be happening?

CHAPTER 6
Moving Forward

. . . .

As I was packing my suitcase to fly back home to attend my mother's funeral, my military buddies gave me a sympathy card and a big hug. It was written all over my face how devastated and sad I was. When I arrived in Buffalo, I rented a car, and I slowly drove home. I was happy to see all of my siblings and the rest of the family, but the main part of the puzzle—my mother—was missing. It wasn't the same.

I didn't even get the chance to tell my mother the whole true story about the assault and Empower.

Pyramid and I are really close, she is much older than I am, and she practically raised me. The older siblings always took care of the younger siblings. There were plenty of times that I wanted to pick up the telephone and call Pyramid and tell her about the assault, the pregnancy, and everything else that happened to me in the military, but she had her own drama. Although Pyramid tried to keep it quiet, she had an abusive husband who beat her on a regular basis.

I told my brother, Zazzle, about Pyramid's abusive husband because I didn't want my sister to be treated like that, she deserved better than that. Zazzle was so livid; he drove to Connecticut, stormed into Pyramid's house, and pistol-whipped Pyramid's husband. Pyramid called my mother to stop Zazzle from shooting her husband. My mother stopped Zazzle from killing Pyramid's husband, but she couldn't stop Zazzle from kicking the man out of his own home. I have seen Zazzle and my other brothers in action; I know what they are capable of doing. That's how I knew what would happen if I ever told them about what Sergeant Cobra did to me. My mother was no longer alive to stop them from going too far, and I did not want any of my brothers to go to jail for the rest of their lives for murdering Sergeant Cobra.

Vegas attended my mother's funeral along with all of my childhood friends. My mother's death was a shock to everyone because it was unexpected. No one knew about Empower, so I asked Vegas not to bring him to my mother's funeral. I didn't want anyone to start asking Vegas a whole bunch of dumb ass questions about Empower or trying to speculate. I know that somebody would have gotten their feelings hurt, so it was best that she didn't bring Empower.

A few days before I went back to my military life, I decided to go to Manhattan to visit Empower and Vegas. A voice—or something inside of me—told me to do the right thing and get my son. I don't know if it was a sign or if it was my mother speaking to me. I am sure that it was my mother speaking to me because that's the type of mother she was, always guiding me the right way—my guardian angel. There is no doubt that if my mother and I would have had our talk, my mother would have told me to go and get Empower. If I didn't get Empower, I know that my mother would have raised him herself.

Vegas had a beautiful home, and she was doing a great job taking care of Empower. But it was time for me to face reality. I told Vegas that I was going to take Empower and raise him by myself.

"Are you sure? Are you ready for this?" she asked me.

"No, I'm not ready, but I have to do what's best for Empower," I told her.

I flew back to my military base to prepare a home for Empower. I applied for family housing, and I received approval right away. The responsiveness and kindness of my commanding officers at this base were in direct contrast to the apathy and abrasive personalities I endured at my previous base.

When I flew back to Manhattan to get Empower, Vegas told me that I could call her anytime I needed her. And, even after Empower and I settled into our new life, Vegas called no less than twice a week to check in on us. I knew she missed Empower, but I also knew she was letting me know I was not in this alone.

VA Services for Military Sexual Trauma:

Help
Hope
Healing

Military Sexual Trauma (MST) refers to sexual assault or harassment experienced during military service. MST includes any unwanted sexual advances and any non-consensual sexual acts committed against you. Anyone can experience MST, regardless of gender. MST can negatively affect a person's mental and physical health, even many years later.

There is no shame in asking for help with your symptoms associated with MST or Post Trauma Stress Disorder (PTSD). It does not make you weak. It takes strength to ask for help. Seeking a counselor or therapist who specializes in sexual trauma can be a good first step to healing.

Resources are available for a veteran struggling with MST

mentalhealth.va.gov/msthome.asp

maketheconnection.net/conditions/military-sexual-trauma

www.womenshealth.va.gov/trauma.asp

CHAPTER 7

Transition
Going Through the Change

· · · · · · · · · · · ·

When I first enlisted in the military, at the age of eighteen, I was bright-eyed and bushy tailed. The whole world was in front of me. Although I had been accepted to lots of colleges, the college life did not appeal to me. I wanted to do something more than just sit in a classroom all day. I was smart, but I knew going to college just was not the path I wanted to take. I was looking for adventure and a way to escape the hometown that felt like it was closing in on me.

When the military recruiter told me about how I could travel the world and learn things the classroom could never teach me, I was hooked. I imagined a long tenure of stellar service, receiving lots of awards and commendations, and rising through the ranks to become a highly decorated officer. I had high hopes of finding the love of my life, having children, and living the American Dream.

Unfortunately for me, the dream turned out to be a nightmare.

After serving my initial term in the military, all I wanted was to get out. With my decision not to re-enlist, I had thirty days before my time in the military would be over.

Here I was at twenty-two years old, thinking about how difficult the transition to civilian life would be. My military career had crashed and burned. My high hopes and dreams of a successful life were dashed. The military had been nothing like I imagined. Four years of active service had felt like a hard forty. I was broken, bruised, and battered. The trauma of my experiences had left me with gaping wounds - deep physical, emotional, mental, and spiritual pain that hurt me to the core.

Yet, even with all of this, I was distressed about leaving. The military had been my livelihood and sole source of survival. I had no idea what I was going to do.

The temptation to give up was overwhelming. I wanted to just curl up in a ball and let it all go. This agony was almost too much to bear. The depression and despair swirled around me and threatened to pull me into a dark abyss.

You are Strong. A small voice whispered to me, reminding me who I am.

I wanted to ignore that voice. My name might be Strong, but in that moment, I felt weak and puny. There was no way I could muscle my way past this calamity. The military had hit me with a right jab of demanding superior officers, a cross of rape and assault, and a left hook of false imprisonment and torture. Now here was the final blow—an uppercut of discharge. This last blow sent me reeling. I was on the mat seeing stars. All I could hear was the referee starting his 10-count.

You are Strong.

The voice continued to speak to me. It got louder and more insistent. With each count of the referee, the voice became clearer.

5...You are Strong.

4...You are Strong.

3...You are Strong.

2...You are Strong.

If it were just all about me, I probably would have continued to ignore the voice. I would have let it all go. It was all too much to handle, and it would be so much easier to give up.

But it wasn't just me.

I had to think about Empower, my beautiful son.

Right before the referee could ring the final bell of defeat, I lifted my head. I was down, but I was not out. I had been hit hard, but I could not let this be a TKO. I had to fight back. Slowly, I got to my feet. I realized that the thirty-day reprieve I had until my discharge went into effect was a perfect time out. It would give me time to recharge and reset. I would be able to develop a plan and come out of my corner, swinging.

Weighing all of my options, I knew I could not go back to Buffalo. Home had not felt the same since my mother died. Although I talked to my family from time to time, I kept them at arm's length. There was no way I could open up to them about the shame and humiliation I endured in the military. There was no way they could ever find out how much of a failure I had become. On the few occasions I did talk to my family, all I heard was how proud they were of me. They thought I was doing so well. The only person who knew the whole truth was Vegas, and she was sworn to secrecy.

I decided to get as far away from my current place as I possibly could. If this was going to work for me, I had to have a fresh new start. Go somewhere no one knew me. That was the only way Empower and I would have a chance to have a happy life.

CHAPTER 8
Unexpected Opportunity
· · · · · · · · · · · ·

I arrived in Spokane with a great expectation. This was my chance at a new beginning. I was determined to do things differently here and make a good life for me and Empower.

With only a high school diploma and four years of military experience, the job prospects in the city were dismal. I pounded the pavement for almost a month looking for a decent job. I would have had a job sooner, but I was not willing to settle for a minimum wage job working at a fast-food restaurant or grocery store. I wanted to be able to provide a good living for my son, giving him all the opportunities he could ever want. I had what I thought was enough savings to cover a month of expenses when I moved to Spokane, but the higher cost of living sucked up my meager resources very quickly. It wasn't long before I had to put a halt to my search for a great job and settle for one that would pay the bills. I ended up working as a clerk at a small retail shop. I had to do whatever it took to survive.

I worked as a clerk in that shop for almost three years, but I never gave up my search for something better. Empower was getting older and more active. I wanted him to participate in sports and other extracurricular activities so he could be exposed to all kinds of new things in life. The money I was making as a clerk was barely covering the current bills we had, and I knew that if I wanted to keep Empower active, I would have to find a new job. Every day after work, I scoured the classified ads for job listings. Most of the good jobs required a college education and lots of experience. I had gained some great customer service and management skills as a clerk. I had even taken a few classes at the Community College. But it seemed as if all the jobs that would elevate me beyond minimum wage were out of reach.

One day, a customer came into the store looking for a birthday gift for his wife. He was frazzled and in a panic. The gift he had planned to give her was not going to be delivered in time, and they had a party planned for that evening. I reassured him that everything would be just fine and asked him about his wife and the kind of gift he wanted to buy. He described his wife to me, told me the colors she preferred and some of the things she liked. It took us more than thirty minutes, but we finally found a gift he thought was perfect for his wife. As I was ringing up his purchases, he smiled and handed me a business card.

"My name is Mr. Energy. I am so grateful I came here. You went above and beyond for me. I could definitely use someone like you on my team. If you are ever looking for a job, call me."

I looked at the card and noticed the name of the company. It was one of the largest companies in the city and one of the ones that I had crossed off my list of possibilities because I never had enough education or experience to apply for their job openings.

"Thank you so much, Mr. Energy," I said nervously. "I am looking for a new job…but I don't think I am qualified to work for your company. I don't have a college degree and I don't have a lot of experience."

"Don't worry about that. I've seen the kind of worker you are. There are some things college can't teach a person. We can train you. Plus, our company has a program that helps our employees get a college education."

"Ok then. I will give you a call. That sounds like just the opportunity I have been looking for."

I was so excited I could barely keep from jumping over the counter to give Mr. Energy a big hug. I contained my emotions enough to wrap up Mr. Energy's purchases and complete the transaction, but I could not keep the huge smile off of my face.

As Mr. Energy left the store, I clutched his card in my hands. I kept looking at the company name and thinking about all the times I had wanted to apply for a job there. This was my big break.

I was up the next morning at six o'clock. I had thought about my interaction with Mr. Energy all night. I couldn't wait to give him a call to find out more about his job offer. I forced myself to remain calm and wait until normal business hours before making the call. At precisely nine o'clock, I dialed Mr. Energy's number.

"Hello, thank you for calling. You've reached Mr. Energy's office. How may I help you?" the cheerful secretary's voice greeted me.

"Hi, my name is Strong. I am calling for an appointment with Mr. Energy to discuss a job opportunity."

"A job opportunity?" she asked in a doubtful tone. "I'm sorry, ma'am. We filled our open positions last week."

"But I just spoke to Mr. Energy yesterday. He told me to give him a call about a job." My heart was pounding so fast, and my mouth was so dry, I could barely get the words out.

The secretary paused for a few moments, then said, "Please give me your number. I will give Mr. Energy a message you called as soon as he gets into the office."

"T-t-thank you," I stammered as I spelled my name and gave the secretary my telephone number.

Why had I gotten my hopes up? Didn't I know things didn't work out for me like that?

Oh well, back to my job search. Since I had the day off, I decided I would use the time to review my resume again and apply to as many positions as I could. I was two hours into my efforts when my phone rang.

"Hello, may I speak to Strong?"

I recognized Mr. Energy's voice immediately. I told myself not to get too excited. He was probably just calling to tell me that he had been mistaken the day before at the store.

"This is Strong," I said hesitantly.

"Hi Strong, I just got your message from my secretary. Thank you for calling so quickly."

"Mr. Energy, I called about the job, but your secretary told me the positions were already filled."

"Yes, we did fill some positions last week. But I have a new position opening that we have not yet posted on the job boards. I wanted to offer it to you."

I was in shock. Dare I get my hopes up? Was my luck finally turning around?

"Ok…what kind of position is it?" I asked.

"You would be working as a direct report to me handling customer support. I liked the way you helped me yesterday. You were kind and very patient. You also knew how to make great recommendations and even got me to spend more than I had planned. I think you would be a great fit for this job. Can you come in for an official interview this week?"

I told Mr. Energy I could come in the next day. He transferred the call to his secretary to schedule the time.

The next day I arrived twenty minutes early to my job interview with Mr. Energy. The secretary who I had been speaking to on the phone greeted me warmly and offered me coffee and pastries. I declined. There was no way I was going to risk spilling anything on my one and only interview suit.

Right on schedule, Mr. Energy came out of his office. Mr. Energy was a short, stout man with a round belly and a big smile. He kind of reminded me of Santa Claus with his bushy gray beard and hearty laugh. Mr. Energy looked over my resume and remarked on how the company valued military experience. When he told me how much the job paid, my jaw almost hit the floor. I would be making nearly three times what I was making at the boutique.

Mr. Energy could barely get the words out before I jumped at the opportunity.

CHAPTER 9
Living THE Dream
· · · · · · · · · · · ·

I spent the next ten years climbing the corporate ladder. Mr. Energy did not lie when he said the company would pay for my college education. And as my direct supervisor, Mr. Energy allowed me to work flexible hours to accommodate my class schedule. I majored in business with an emphasis in accounting and finance. As Mr. Energy was promoted through the company's ranks, he brought me along with him. When Mr. Energy was named the Vice President of Operations, he promoted me to a senior management position on his team. I had gone from minimum wage to a six-figure salary.

As Empower grew older, I was able to give him all of the things he ever needed and mostly all of the things he wanted. There were some things I just wouldn't buy, especially tennis shoes for three hundred dollars, no matter how much money I was making. My salary allowed us to live a very comfortable life. I did not have to pinch pennies or have to shop at discount stores. I was able to put Empower in all kinds of activities, go on family vacations, and eat at great restaurants. I was even able to save money and buy a big four-bedroom house. That house was my castle, and I treated it with the utmost care.

With my last promotion, I was now making enough money to afford my dream car, a silver 500E Mercedes Benz. Every time I sat behind the wheel in that luxurious vehicle, I knew I had finally made it.

Although I was still distant from my family, we talked occasionally. When they learned about the success I was having with my career and my numerous promotions, they would call and ask for money from time to time. I did not mind helping out. In fact, I loved being able to share my good fortune with them. I always felt a little bit guilty for not telling them about Empower and my traumatic experiences in the military. Helping them with a few hundred dollars here or there was one way I could let them know I still cared about them.

The only part of my life I wanted more in was my love life. Being a good mom was important to me. I put all of my free time and energy into being the best mother I could possibly be for Empower. Running around to sports practices and other extracurricular activities, being a PTA mom, and making room for our special mother-son time, on top of my work and school schedule, did not give me much time for anything else. Dating was the last thing on my mind.

Plus, I was still very traumatized by my military experiences. After what Sergeant Cobra had done to me, I was leery of allowing anyone to get too close. It not only affected my romantic relationships, but it also prevented me from making friends. I was pleasant at work and offered help when needed, but I did not socialize with my co-workers outside of work. Several times over the years, various co-workers would invite me to parties or other events. I would always decline. Soon, they just stopped asking me. The closest person I had to a friend at work was Premier, Mr. Energy's secretary turned office manager. Mr. Energy was very loyal to his employees. He made sure that his team members were the first to be considered whenever opportunities for promotion were available. Premier and I occasionally talked during lunch. She even gave me her telephone number and told me to call her if I ever wanted to hang out on the weekends. I never took her up on her offer, but I did appreciate having someone I could trust in the office. Trust did not come easy for me. I could count on three fingers the number of people I trusted even a little bit. Having Premier as one of them was a big help to me.

One day as I was eating my lunch at one of the outside tables in the company's courtyard, a man came up to me and introduced himself.

"Hi, my name is Golden."

I looked at him in surprise. Most people in the office knew that I ate lunch alone most days; I had been anti-social long enough that no one ever attempted to sit with me anymore.

I nodded my head and said, "Nice to meet you."

Immediately, I turned back to the book I was reading. I hoped he would get the hint that I did not want to be bothered.

"What's your name?" he asked, interrupting me again.

Apparently, he did not get the hint. I did not want to be rude, but I was not interested in having a conversation with this man.

"My name is Strong," I said, not even bothering to look up this time.

"That's a nice name, Strong. Can I sit with you?"

What? Why did he want to sit with me?

I looked around the courtyard and saw at least three open tables. I pointed to one of them and said, "This table is taken. There is plenty of room at that table over there."

"I think the view is nicer over here," he said with a smile.

I put my book down and decided that since being nice wasn't working, I would have to be direct and let him know I was not interested in him.

I had seen this man around the office a few times, and I admit he was very nice looking. Golden had a crisp, clean, professional appearance. Every time I saw him, I noticed how well he dressed. His dark black wavy hair was cut short, and he had hazel eyes with a combination of green, gold, and brown coloring. He was over six feet tall, and from my seated position, he towered over me like a giant.

I looked up at him and said, "I do not want you to sit with me. I like to enjoy lunch by myself. Please find another table."

This time I did not look away. I kept staring at him in hopes he would just leave. Thankfully, he did.

"Ok," he said as he smiled and walked away.

I sighed in relief and started to read my book again. Then, I heard a scraping sound. When I looked up to see what had made the noise, I saw Golden pulling one of the nearby tables. He pushed the table right next to mine and sat down.

When I glared at him with my best evil stare, he just smirked. This guy was definitely persistent and creative. Despite myself, I smiled.

"You must think you are funny," I said, trying to hide my amusement.

He laughed and said, "My mama always told me, when you want something, go after it."

"Really? And what is it that you want?" I was surprised at the flirty tone of my voice.

Was I really flirting with this man?

"I want to get to know you, Ms. Strong." He said. "I've seen you around the office, and hopefully, you will let me see you outside of the office."

I shook my head. I had to put my guard back up and nip this in the bud before it went any further.

"No, thank you. I am not interested," I said firmly.

"Why not?"

"I do not have to have a reason. I am just not interested."

Golden shrugged his shoulders and said, "Ok."

For the rest of my lunch break, I was on edge. Golden didn't say another word to me. He ate his lunch as I read my book. When my break was over, I got up and went back to my office and tried to work. My mind was distracted though. I thought about Golden and him asking me out. He seemed like a nice guy, but I did not want to get too close to him.

After that day, I saw Golden around the office more and more. Every time we passed each other in the hallway, he would smile; I would look the other way.

A few weeks later, I was in my usual solitary spot in the court-yard eating my lunch. It was Friday afternoon. The week had been more hectic than usual and I needed my solitary time to decompress. Ever since the day Golden had infiltrated my space, I made sure to find the table in the furthest corner and I sat with my back to all of the other tables in the courtyard. About fifteen minutes into my break, I felt a tap on my shoulder.

I turned around to see Golden with a bag in his hand. This time he didn't ask if he could join me. He just pulled out the chair on the left side of me and sat down. The tables were large enough to seat four people, but with Golden's large presence invading my space, the table seemed much smaller.

"Hey, Strong," he said. "How is your day going?"

"Why are you sitting here?" I asked. "Can't you find somewhere else to sit?"

"Nope. It's my lucky day. All of the other tables are full," he said with a twinkle in his eyes.

I looked around the courtyard and saw that he was right. It was a bright sunny day, and it seemed as if everyone in the company had decided to eat lunch outside. My table was the only one with extra chairs.

"You could have chosen to eat inside," I said.

"I could have, but then I would have missed the chance to eat lunch with you."

I tried to ignore Golden as I opened my book again. If I didn't say anything to him, maybe he would eat his lunch and let me finish my break in peace.

No such luck.

"What are you reading?"

I silently held up the book so he could see the cover. I kept reading.

"Looks interesting. What is it about?"

Obviously, I was not going to be able to enjoy my break in peace. Without saying a word, I started to get up to go into my office for a few more moments of quiet before I had to get back to work. As

I pushed my chair in, I felt Golden's hand on mine.

"Why are you always giving me the cold shoulder?" he asked.

"Look, you are nice and all, but I am not interested."

Before I could walk away, he handed me a piece of paper and said, "I would really like to get to know you better. Take my number and call me if you ever change your mind."

I took the piece of paper and slipped it into my pocket. As soon as I got to my office, I would throw it away. As I got off of the elevator on my department's floor, Premier saw me and smiled.

She winked at me and said, "I saw you and Golden eating lunch together in the courtyard."

"We were not eating lunch together. He just sat at my table because there was no room anywhere else."

"I think he likes you. He is a great guy. I think you should go out with him," Premier advised.

I looked at Premier and shook my head. I knew that Golden was a good guy. Everyone in the office seemed to like him, and he appeared to be kind to all of his employees. Even with me being outside of the gossip circle, I knew that several of the office ladies had a crush on him.

"No, thank you. I'm good." I told Premier as I walked into my office and closed the door.

The next day, as I checked my pants pockets before I sent my clothes to the dry cleaner's, I found the piece of paper Golden had given me. I unfolded the paper and looked at his number. Instead of throwing the paper away as I intended, I put it on my dresser. Maybe Premier was right. Perhaps I should take a chance and go out with Golden.

Golden's telephone number sat on my dresser for the rest of the week. When he saw me in the office, he still smiled at me, but he didn't try to eat lunch with me anymore.

The following week, I was sitting on my bed watching television. Empower was away at a two-week summer sports camp. I had the house all to myself. I looked at my dresser and saw the piece of paper with Golden's telephone number on it. I had looked at it every day for the past few weeks; every time I did, I wondered how it would feel to go on a date with him.

A little voice in my head said, Go ahead. Give him a call.

I got up and picked up the piece of paper. I started to dial Golden's number then hung up. I realized I did want to call him, but I was scared. It had been a long time since I went on a date and I was not sure if I could do it. Since Sergeant Cobra violated me, I had only been out with a few guys, and I always cut it off very quickly because I just didn't know who I could trust.

I took a deep breath and decided to give it a try.

I dialed the number. When Golden answered, I was silent for a long time.

"Hello?" he said for the third time.

"Hi…this is Strong," I said very quietly.

Now his end of the line was silent.

Finally, he said, "Strong?" with a question in his voice.

"Yeah, it's me. You…you gave me your number…I decided to call." I said, trying not to show how nervous I was.

"Wow. What a great surprise. I didn't think you would ever call me."

After a few moments, my nerves calmed. Golden and I talked for several hours. It turned out we had a lot of things in common. He was hilarious and made me laugh. I felt at ease with a man for the first time in as long as I could remember. He asked if I would go out with him and I said yes. My only stipulation was that no one in the company could know about us dating. There was no policy against the company's employees dating each other, but I didn't want anyone in my business.

Golden agreed to keep our relationship private, and we started dating. It took me a few months before I introduced him to my son. Empower was very protective of me, and I was hesitant to bring a man into his life. I had nothing to worry about though. As soon as Empower met Golden, they hit it off. Golden went with me to all of Empower's football and basketball games, and he hung out with Empower, talking about sports and giving him manly advice about growing up.

As time passed, I began to settle into my good life. Golden and I continued to date. Empower grew up to be an amazing young man, going to college and then enlisting in the military as an officer. I continued to excel in my career. I felt blessed and on top of the world.

But I should have known it wouldn't last.

CHAPTER 10
The Main Event
· · · · · · · · · · · ·

One Monday morning on the way to work, I went to Winchell's to buy donuts for my co-workers. Although I still did not socialize with them outside of the office and I still ate lunch by myself almost every day, I had thawed out a bit and was congenial enough to speak in the hallways and engage in some friendly conversations from time to time. I would probably never be comfortable enough to trust any of them, other than Premier and Golden, to share my personal business; but it was nice to walk through the hallways without scowling and giving everyone the cold shoulder.

As soon as I stepped off the elevator onto the fifth floor, I noticed a frenzy of activity. People were rushing by and running around as if someone had pulled the fire alarm.

"What's going on?" I asked Premier as I walked into the break room and placed the three boxes of donuts on the corner table next to the coffee maker.

"You didn't see the email?" she asked.

"No, I just got in."

"They have called an emergency department meeting. It is at nine in the conference room. Seems like it's going to be a big deal. Rumors are flying around that something major is about to happen. Some people are nervous." Premier responded as she flitted around, organizing the breakroom counter.

I just shrugged at Premier's comments. Our company had made several changes over the past few years; none of the changes had been bad.

"I don't think we have anything to worry about." I said, walking out of the break room, heading to my office.

As I entered my office, I looked at the clock—8:35. I had a few moments to relax and get settled in for the day before the meeting started. I sat down at my desk and turned on my computer. I looked over my schedule for the day. I had a few meetings and client calls, but other than that, I was free. I could probably leave the office early today so I could get in a few extra hours of studying done for the new Master's program I enrolled in. The semester had just started and I liked to stay ahead.

I sat back in my chair to finish my coffee and donut before the meeting. Gratitude flowed through me as I thought about how great it was to be able to work at such a great company. I was taking the last bite of my donut when my office telephone rang. Swallowing quickly, I answered.

"Good morning. This is Strong. How may I help you?"

"Hi, Strong." Mr. Energy said. "Please come to my office for a moment."

"On my way, sir," I chirped. I was in a great mood and always happy to see Mr. Energy.

Before heading to Mr. Energy's office, I stopped by the break room to pick up a few donuts and a cup of coffee for him. He usually got into the office very early and I knew he skipped breakfast most days.

As I walked in the door, I placed the donuts and coffee on his desk and took a seat.

"Thank you, Strong. This is a great treat." Mr. Energy said, biting into one of the donuts.

He took a sip of coffee then continued, "Have you heard about the department meeting this morning?"

"Yes, Premier told me when I arrived. I will be there."

"Good. I just wanted to talk to you a bit before we head into the meeting. I do not want you to be surprised."

"Premier said the meeting was about some kind of company changes…" I said. "When I got here, everyone was running around acting nervous. But I am not worried. We have had company changes before."

Mr. Energy just nodded. He took a bite of the second donut and chewed it slowly. He took another sip of his coffee then took a deep breath before continuing.

"Strong, I am leaving the company."

I sat in shock. There were a million thoughts running through my mind but no words came out.

When I did not respond, Mr. Energy kept talking, "It's time for me to slow down and take it easy. My wife and I are moving to Texas to be near our children and I have decided to take a job that is a lot less involved so we can enjoy our grandbabies."

I was definitely not expecting this. Mr. Energy had been my mentor and advisor throughout my entire time at the company. I could not imagine working there without him.

I felt myself getting choked up. Mr. Energy saw the tears in my eyes and he said, "It's going to be okay. You have grown so much since you have been here. You are a great worker and I know you will continue to be an asset to this company."

"Who's going to take your place?" I asked, knowing there was no one who could ever do as good a job as Mr. Energy had done all these years.

Mr. Energy was quiet for a moment, then he said, "This is what will be announced in the meeting today. Please don't tell anyone before it starts."

I rolled my eyes. Mr. Energy knew I barely spoke to the other people in the office.

"I will not tell anyone," I said.

"Ok...I will tell you...Edge will be moving up to replace me. He will be the new Vice President of Operations for the company."

I blinked several times. I could not believe what I was hearing.

"E-E-Edge?" I stammered.

"Yes, Edge." Mr. Energy confirmed. "I know he has an abrasive personality at times, but I think you of all people can relate to that. Edge has the experience and background to do the job. He's been here for quite some time, and he has shown that he can handle the responsibility."

I just nodded. I personally did not like Edge. There was just something about him that made my skin crawl. Not only was he a brown noser and kiss ass, but he also had a reputation around the office for being a womanizer. Premier had told me that he had affairs with several of the ladies in our department and other departments in the company. I did not think he would be a good replacement for Mr. Energy, but who was I to tell them how to run the company?

***

Edge's transition as Vice President of Operations and the head of our department was a bit rocky at first. We all missed Mr. Energy. But it was more than that. Mr. Energy trusted all of us to do our jobs well. He gave us assignments then gave us the freedom to manage them the way we saw fit. Edge was not like that at all. He was a micromanager, and he continuously looked over our shoulders. Whereas Mr. Energy had a monthly staff meeting to check in on the progress of our projects, Edge held weekly meetings. Each of us was required to have a detailed report of our projects and what we had accomplished during the week. Edge also required us to send him daily emails about what we were doing. It was a nightmare. We spent more time doing reports than our actual jobs. On top of that, the extra work duties gave me less time to study and complete my master's program assignments. I was tired and worn out.

When Christmas time came around, I was glad. I had never before craved to have time off from my job the whole time I worked at the company, but I needed a break this year. Thankfully, the company closed its offices the day before Christmas to the Monday after New Year's Day.

I looked at my calendar. It was Friday; exactly three work days left before Christmas Eve. I just had to make it through Monday, Tuesday, and Wednesday of the following week, and I would be free.

As I was shutting down my computer and clearing my desk for the day, I heard a knock on my office door. I looked up and saw Edge standing in the doorway.

"Hello. How can I help you?" I asked in a cool voice.

I still did not like Edge. He had shown over the past few months that he was a horrible boss.

"I look forward to seeing you tonight at the Christmas Party," he said.

Our company's annual Christmas Party was that evening. In all of my years working at the company, I had never attended the company Christmas Party, and I did not plan to start this year.

"I will not be attending the Christmas Party," I said, straightening a few files on my desk.

"This year, attendance is mandatory for all employees." Edge said.

"What? How can it be mandatory? It's a party!" I exclaimed.

"It's a new policy for our department. We want to make sure that everyone develops as a team. I expect to see you there."

Without another word, Edge walked out of my office.

I immediately picked up my office telephone and called Premier.

When she answered, I said, "Did you know the Christmas Party was mandatory this year?"

"Yeah...there was a memo sent out a few hours ago. Didn't you see it.?"

"No, I was caught up in a project. I didn't check my emails before I closed down my computer."

"Hold on, I'm coming to your office."

A few moments later, Premier walked into my office with a sheet of paper. She handed the paper to me, and I read it.

The memo was short and had only a few sentences. It said exactly what Edge had told me. The Christmas Party was a mandatory team-building activity this year. We all were required to attend.

"I can't believe this!" I growled.

"I know…you've never been to the company Christmas Party before. People are going to be shocked to see you there. Most people in the company think you vanish at night or something because we never see you outside of the office."

I knew Premier was trying to get me to laugh, but I was not in a joking mood. I had no desire to go to the Christmas Party.

Sighing, I crumpled up the piece of paper and threw it into the trash can

After Premier left my office, I called Golden.

"Hey, did you see the memo about the Christmas Party?"

"Yeah," he said, coughing. "I was going to call you and see if you saw it," he managed to get out before he started coughing again.

"I didn't see it at first, but Edge came by my office and told me that I had to attend. Then Premier showed me the memo. You okay?" I asked him as he kept coughing into the phone.

"I'm fine. Just a bit of a cold, I think. Are you going to the party?"

"I don't have a choice. I will show up and stay for a little while. Are you going?"

"I'll be there. I know you don't want people to know we are together, but hopefully, you will at least talk to me there," he said, laughing.

"I'll talk to you. But I am not going to let you get too close. That cough sounds horrible. I don't want you to give me your cooties."

We laughed for a bit, and then I hung up. I had planned on taking a long bubble bath and curling up with a good book, but I guess that would have to wait.

* * *

The company rented a lovely event venue for the party. There were twinkle lights all over and several tall Christmas trees were beautifully decorated in the corners of the room. There was lots of food and an open bar. A DJ was playing music from one corner of the large dance floor. A few chairs and tables were scattered around the room, but most people were standing in small groups, mingling.

I looked around the room and saw Premier standing with a few people from our department. Deciding to jump right in, I walked over and greeted them.

My co-workers looked shocked.

"Wow! I definitely didn't expect to see you here. I know they made it mandatory, but I just knew you would find a way not to come," one of them said.

"I'm here, but I am not staying long. I just want them to see I came and then I am leaving."

Premier took my hand and spun me around.

"Girl, you clean up nice. I love that dress and those shoes."

My dress was a simple black dress that fell just above my knees. Although the high neckline did not reveal any cleavage, the dress fit me well and showed off my curves. My shoes were three-inch black and silver stilettos with rhinestones. I knew my co-workers were not used to seeing me in anything but pantsuits and low heels. This was definitely a surprise for them.

We engaged in small talk for a few more moments. Golden had not yet arrived and I kept looking at the door to make sure I would not miss him when he came in.

When the co-workers that Premier and I were talking to stepped away to get food, Premier turned to me and said, "You looking for you man?'

"Shhh." I scolded her. "Don't say that here."

"I know...I know. You don't want anyone to know you two are dating. Girl, it's been years. You really should stop trying to hide that."

"It is none of anyone's business. No one knows and I want to keep it that way."

My phone buzzed and I looked down to see a text from Golden. He was sick and was not going to make it.

I showed Premier the text message and said, "I knew that cold was bad. When we talked earlier it sounded like he was coughing up a lung."

"Well, I guess you are just stuck with me all night. Do you want to get some food or a drink?"

"In a minute. I'm going to go to the restroom then I will meet you near the food tables."

Finishing up in the restroom, I headed to meet Premier near the food table. Halfway there, Edge stepped out in front of me.

"You look really good tonight," he said, winking at me.

I could tell he was intoxicated, and I did not want to spend any time talking to him. I might have to be at this party, but I did not have to engage in a conversation with him.

As I walked away, I heard Edge make a few sexual comments about how he wanted to take my dress off and the things he wanted to do to me.

I shook it off and kept going. Edge was definitely under the influence, and it would be best for me to stay far away from him.

I remember the last time I had been in close quarters with an intoxicated man, and things had not turned out so good.

Premier and I ate. She tried to get me to get a drink, but I declined. After another hour, my feet were hurting, and I was ready to go. I told Premier I would see her in the office on Monday and said goodbye to the few co-workers that were standing near us.

I grabbed my coat from the coat room and headed for the elevator. Before the door closed, an arm reached in to stop it. It was Edge.

"Where are you going?" he asked.

"It's time for me to go."

He stepped on the elevator with me and stood very close.

I shrank into the corner as far away from him as I could. I looked at the numbers on the elevator and prayed that we would get to the bottom floor quickly.

Suddenly the elevator jerked and the lights flashed off.

Edge pushed close to me and grabbed my face. He pressed his body onto mine and then he kissed me. I struggled against him and tried to get him to stop, but he was really strong.

The elevator sputtered again and the lights flickered back on and kept moving to the bottom floor. A few seconds later, the door opened and I ran out of the elevator.

"You are such a creep. Stay away from me before I call the cops."

Edge came up to me and said, "You won't tell anyone about this or you will be sorry."

A strong sense of déjà vu came over me.

Don't tell anyone.

What was it about crazy men and their threats? If they didn't want people to know how devious they were, they should stop their horrible behavior.

I ran to my car and drove straight home, shaking all the way. I decided this was not going to be like last time. I was going to tell someone what Edge had done to me.

I called Golden, but he didn't answer.

The next day, I called Premier and told her what Edge had done.

"That bastard!" she said.

We talked about it for a bit longer, and I told her that I would go to Human Resources first thing Monday morning.

CHAPTER 11
Wicked Workplace

· · · · · · · · · · · ·

As soon as I arrived in the building on Monday morning, I headed straight to the Human Resources Department. I knew that I could not be silent about what Edge had done to me. I was no longer that scared girl who allowed Sergeant Cobra to go unpunished. I was a grown woman and I valued myself enough now to speak up. My conversation with Premier and her encouraging words had given me the push I needed to take this step.

When I entered the Human Resources Specialist's office, I immediately told him everything that happened after the Christmas Party. I told him how Edge had followed me onto the elevator and forced himself on me when the elevator stopped.

"Where you drinking at the Christmas Party?" the HR Specialist asked.

"Was I drinking?" I asked, confused by his questions. "No. I was not drinking. What does that have to do with what I just told you?"

"I am just trying to get the whole story. There was an open bar at the party and many people drank more than their share."

"Sir, I do not drink. What I told you was the whole story."

"What were you wearing at the party?"

"Excuse me? What was I wearing? Why are you asking me these questions? I am telling you that a man, one of this company's employees, assaulted me and you are asking me what I was wearing?"

"Yes…please don't get irate. We just need to get all of the facts so we can find out what really happened."

"What really happened? I just told you everything that happened. Don't you believe me?"

His response was another question, "Did you speak to or interact with Edge while you were at the party?"

"He came over to me at the party and made rude comments about my dress."

"What did your dress look like?"

"With all due respect, the way my dress looked has nothing to do with this. I want to report the inappropriate behavior and sexual harassment of one of your employees, but it seems as if you want to accuse me. Is there someone else I can talk to?"

"No, ma'am. I am the HR Specialist in charge of employee complaints. I will take what you have told me and do an investigation into the matter. We will follow up with you after the holiday."

He put the form he'd been filling out on top of a pile of papers on his desk. Then he turned to me and said, "Thank you for coming in. We will let you know when we have decided."

I left the office feeling dejected. Apparently, he didn't believe me or, if he did believe me, he was not going to really do anything about it. I went back to my office and tried to focus on the tasks I needed to complete before the Christmas break. If Human Resources failed to do anything about this, I would talk to someone else.

* * *

Two weeks after the Christmas break and there was still no answer from Human Resources about my complaint. My calls to inquire about the progress of the investigation went unanswered. I left at least three voicemail messages with the HR Specialist who had taken my complaint. He had yet to return any of my calls. I decided that if I had not heard anything by the following week, I was going to talk to the Human Resources Director.

I was just about to go on my lunch break when I heard a knock on my office door. Our department manager, my immediate direct supervisor, and two security guards stood in my doorway.

"May I help you?" I asked.

The manager walked into my office and said, "Strong, you are being let go. Your position has been terminated, effective immediately. Please gather your belongings and turn in your employee badge."

I was being fired? How could this be? After working at this company for more than two decades, I was now being let go. Every performance review I have ever had with this company was stellar. I was not ever late. I rarely even took a sick day. There was no way they could fire me.

"What? Why?" I stammered.

"Strong, your position has been terminated," he repeated.

"What does that mean? How can my position be terminated?"

"I am just delivering the news to you. These security officers are here to help you gather your belongings and escort you from the building."

My head started spinning and I felt nauseous. This was so unexpected. I never would have imagined that something like this would happen.

I immediately thought of Edge and my complaint with the Human Resources Department.

"Is this because I made a sexual harassment complaint against Edge?" I asked angrily.

"Strong, your position has been terminated," he repeated. That is all he would say.

Seeing that there was no choice but for me to comply with what he was saying, I picked up my purse and lunch bag. I looked around the office. I had not personalized this office with any of my things, so there was nothing else to gather.

I unclipped my employee identification badge from my key chain and placed it on the desk. I knew angry words and violent rage were not going to help me. Plus, I did not want to make a scene. I had spent all of my time at this company making sure no one was privy to my personal business. I was not going to let them see me go ballistic and have something to gossip about.

As I walked through the parking garage to my car, I looked up and said, "Lord, I am putting this situation in Your hands."

* * *

I cried for days, going over and over in my mind what happened. All I could come up with was that Edge and the HR Specialist were in cahoots. The Good Old Boy Network had totally screwed me. My track record at the company meant nothing. All of the hard work I put in was not even a factor. They determined I was a problem and I had to go.

I thought about Mr. Energy. Something like this would have never happened while he was at the company. I know he believed Edge was the right person for the job, but the company had made a huge mistake by giving Edge so much power in the company. If he did this to me, there was no telling what he had done before or what he would do to others after me.

Knowing that this situation just was not right, I searched for an attorney. She listened to me and said, "You have a good basis for a case. But I will be honest with you. It could take several months or maybe even years to resolve. Do you still want to proceed?"

"Yes. I want to hold these people accountable. I don't want this to happen to someone else."

The attorney told me her fees and I agreed to come to her office to sign the papers necessary to start the process.

In the meantime, I had to start looking for a new job. I was so glad that Empower was out of the house and living his own life. But I still had a lot of bills to pay each month. My mortgage, car payment, utilities, food—the bills would not stop coming just because I lost my job.

I scoured the job boards and classified ads. It had been a long time since I had to search for a job, but I felt as if I was in a much better position this time. I had a college degree and lots of experience under my belt. I updated my resume and submitted it to every opportunity that looked promising.

In the months that followed, I submitted my resume to several companies. Every day I would search the job boards and classified ads. I submitted at least ten resumes a week, but nothing came through. My bills were piling up. I was three months behind on my mortgage and car payments. My phone was constantly ringing with bill collectors calling to demand I pay them. I could barely afford to buy groceries, and I had several final notices from the utility companies.

I asked friends and family members back home—the ones I had given money to so many times over the years—but none of them would help me. Premier kept calling, but I did not answer any of her calls. I did not want to face anyone at the company that had betrayed me.

me too.

#MeToo is a movement of survivors and their supporters, powered by courage, determined to end sexual violence and harassment. One of the biggest effects of the #MeToo Movement has been to show Americans and the people around the world how widespread sexual harassment, assault, and other misconduct really are.

As more and more survivors spoke out, they learned they are not alone. And people who had never had cause to think about sexual harassment before suddenly saw how much it had affected their co-workers, children, parents, and friends.

www.metoomvmt.org

CHAPTER 12
Slammed Doors

· · · · · · · · · · · ·

I lost everything.

My castle - the beautiful home I adored - was taken away from me in foreclosure.

My car - that dream car that was the symbol of my achievements - was repossessed.

My livelihood - the job that had meant so much to me - was ripped from my hands and I still had not found anything to replace it.

Nine months after losing my job, I was destitute and homeless.

After getting the foreclosure notice, I devised a plan to help me get the money to pay the balance owed so I could hold on a little bit longer until I found a job. I gathered up my jewelry and other items I thought would bring good money and took it all to the pawnshop. I did not get nearly what I thought I would. I had a yard sale to sell some of my furniture and other belongings. That was a joke. I sold some things but only made a couple hundred dollars. With the money I had gotten from the pawnshop, I was still so far away from my goal. Then, I had the bright idea to go to the casino and take the few dollars I did have to hit the jackpot. But that was the day my car was repossessed.

It seemed as if everything was against me. The entire universe was conspiring to keep me down.

I lost the fight to pay back my mortgage and had to leave my house and most of my belongings behind. There was no place to take them. With the money I made from the pawnshop and yard sale, I had enough money to stay in a hotel for a couple of weeks.

The last day of my hotel stay, I knew I had hit rock bottom. There was no place for me to go. I had run out of money and run out of options. With the cold, snowy weather outside, I knew I would not make it if I had to sleep on the streets. I went to the WES Office, dragging the few personal belongings I had that could fit into suitcases. I didn't have money to catch the bus, so I walked the two miles from the hotel to the downtown office in the cold, dragging my bags behind me. I arrived at the office cold, tired, and hungry.

I walked into the building and looked around. It was filled with people who looked just like me, broken and in despair. I walked up to the reception desk and said, "I need help."

The clerk looked at me and smirked, "So does everyone else in here. Take a number and have a seat."

I was taken aback by his rude tone. There was no compassion in his voice at all. How could someone be so mean?

I walked over to the ticket stand and pulled a number.

"Number 55." I heard a voice say over the intercom system.

I looked down at my ticker - number 112. I just shook my head. I was going to be here all day. At least it was warm inside the building.

I rolled my bags over to the only chair available. It was in a corner next to a large woman with several kids. All of them had bags of chips and snacks. I heard my stomach growl. The woman noticed me eyeing her chips and offered me some.

Before she could get out the words, I said yes and took the bag from her. This was the first thing I had to eat in almost two days.

After waiting four hours, my number was finally called. I gathered my bags and followed a short, blonde woman to a tiny cubicle. There was barely enough room for us to sit. There was no extra space for me to wheel my bags in.

"Put those against the wall and have a seat," she said, pointing to a tiny corner across from her cubicle.

When I sat down, I told her I needed assistance because I had lost my job, my home, my car, and I did not have any food to eat. She looked at me with the same look the man at the front desk had given me.

They really needed to think about doing some kind of training for their workers or at least hire people who had hearts.

Without any words and a scowl on her face, she handed me a stack of forms and told me to fill them out. I answered all of the questions and gave her back the forms. She entered my information into her computer systems and then turned to me.

"We cannot offer you assistance."

"Why not?" I asked. Surely, there was something that could be done to help me.

"Your tax records show that you made too much money over the past year to qualify for any of our services."

"But I have been out of work for nine months. I don't have any money. My house and car have been taken. I am homeless. You have got to help me."

"I am sorry, ma'am. There is nothing we can do for you here," she said, not sounding sorry at all.

"What am I supposed to do?"

"If you really have no place to go, I suggest you try the women's shelter. It is a few blocks from here."

I snapped. All day I had waited patiently in this building. I was starving. I was homeless. I had no place to go. And here this woman was with her patronizing tone telling me there was nothing she could do to help me.

How could I not qualify for assistance? I had nothing.

I stood up and started yelling, "How can you do this to me? This is a place where people are supposed to come to get help and you sit there at your desk and tell me there is nothing you can do to help me."

"Ma'am…Ma'am…calm down before I call security."

"Call them! Tell them how you are treating me. I bet you have a nice place to stay and food to eat. Well, I don't! I have nothing and no one is willing to help me."

Noticing the commotion, a security guard approached the cubicle. Before he could say a word, I grabbed my bags and dragged them behind me as I stomped to the door. Several sets of eyes followed me as I made my way out of the building. At that point, I couldn't care less about what they were thinking of me.

I walked to the women's shelter and went inside. I told the receptionist at the front desk that I was homeless and needed a place to stay. She told me that the shelter was at full capacity that day and there was no room for anyone else.

What? This was my last option before having to sleep on the street tonight.

I banged my fist on the receptionist's desk and shouted, "Where am I supposed to sleep tonight? I have no place to go!"

A big burly lady came through the side door of the main lobby and approached me.

"What is going on here?" she asked in a loud, commanding voice.

I could tell this woman was used to being in charge.

"I need a place to stay. I don't have anywhere else to go."

She told me the same thing the receptionist said, "There is no room here at this time. You must leave and stop causing a scene."

With hot tears flowing down my face, I slammed my hand on the desk again, kicked the trash can, and stormed out of the building.

I could not believe this. The people that were supposed to be able to help me turned me away.

Not knowing where to go, I walked down the street. On top of being tired, cold, and hungry, I was now scared. Soon the sun would go down and it would be dark. Where would I sleep? Would it be safe? What if someone tried to take my belongings? Or worse, what if someone tried to harm me?

My stomach was still rumbling loudly when I saw a McDonald's in front of me. I saw a few people getting out of their car to go into the restaurant. I had always helped homeless people asking for money in the past. Now, it was time for me to swallow my pride and ask for more help.

I prayed that these people would not be like the people at the WES office and the shelter. Hopefully, they would show some compassion and give me money for food. If I had to sleep on the street tonight, I needed something to eat.

As I approached the couple, I saw the woman give me a sideways look.

Gathering up my courage, I said, "Please help me. I need money to buy food."

The man looked at me and for the first time in a long time I saw someone willing to help me.

He gave me a five-dollar bill and said, "God bless you."

There were still good people in the world.

I went inside the restaurant and ordered two cheeseburgers, fries, and water. I took my food to a table in the back and ate slowly. I did not know how long it would be until my next meal. I stayed in the restaurant as long as I could. When they were finally about to close, I knew I could not stay any longer.

I walked outside with my bags. It was totally dark and the night air was very cold. I could tell that the temperature would go below freezing. Walking down the street, I looked around for places where I could stop for the night. A few blocks down, I saw a park with a playground and several picnic tables and benches.

I went over to one of the tables and sat down. I put my bags under the table and just stared at the night sky. I was shivering from the cold. My coat was not going to be enough to keep me warm. Seeing no other choice, I laid my head on the picnic table and closed my eyes. Tonight I would sleep here and tomorrow I would try again to find some place warm to stay.

Just as I was about to drift off to sleep, I heard loud footsteps behind me.

My head popped up and my heart started pounding in my chest. I looked around to see if there was anything I could use as a weapon to protect myself.

"Ma'am, you can't sleep here." a man with a gruff voice said.

I turned around to see a police officer standing behind me. He was a tall, muscular man, and he had the same look on his face that I had seen so many times that day.

When I did not respond, the officer repeated, "Ma'am, you cannot sleep here. This park is closed to the public at night."

"Is it closed to the public or just closed to the homeless?" I retorted in anger.

The officer looked me over and pulled out his walkie talkie. I heard him calling for backup. Then he asked me if I had any identification on me.

I did not understand why I needed identification to be in the park, but I had seen enough news stories about police officers to know that I should just follow along.

I riffled through my bag, looking for my identification. I had all of my important papers in that bag and it was a total mess. As I was looking through the papers, the office said, "Ma'am are you a veteran?"

I looked down to see that some of the paperwork from my military service was showing. I said, "I guess so. I served in the military for four years."

"Why are you out here? What happened?" he asked. There was a softness to his voice now.

I told him the whole story of how I was fired from my job and couldn't find another one. I told him about my house being foreclosed on and my car being repossessed. Then, I told him how after I had run out of money to stay in hotels, I had gone to the WES office for help but could not qualify for assistance. I told him about the ladies at the women's shelter who told me there was no room.

"I have nowhere else to go," I said.

As I was finishing my story, a female officer approached us. I guess she was the backup he had called.

The two officers stepped away and had a long conversation. I could not hear everything they said, but I could tell they were trying to figure out what to do with me.

"Get your bags and come with us," the female officer commanded.

Nervously, I asked, "Are you taking me to jail?"

Thoughts of the Stockade I had been taken to after Sergeant Cobra's assault flashed through my mind. I definitely didn't want to relive an experience like that. But I thought about the fact that jail would be warmer than sleeping on a park bench. At least I would have a bed and maybe some food.

"No, we are taking you to get some help," the male officer responded.

I couldn't believe what he was saying. Where was he going to take me to get some help at this time of night?

Deciding wherever they were taking me would be better than staying in the cold, I followed them to a police car. The male officer took my bags and put them into the trunk. Then he opened the back door of the police car and told me to get in. I hesitated for a moment. The last time I was in a police car, things had not gone so well.

The male officer got into the driver's seat and drove away from the park, with the female officer in her car following behind us.

We drove for a few minutes and then he said, "Let's go."

He opened the back door of the car, and I looked around. We were in front of the women's shelter.

"They are not going to help me here. They already told me to leave earlier today."

"Don't worry about that. Just come with me."

When we walked inside the building, the same receptionist was sitting at the desk. She gave me a harsh look then turned to the two officers standing beside me.

"How can I help you, officers?"

The male officer walked up to the desk and said, "We need to see Angel."

The receptionist picked up the phone on her desk and made a call. A few moments later, a slender black woman with long braided hair came into the lobby area.

"Officer Lifesaver, it is good to see you," she said cheerfully. "What can I do for you this evening?"

The officer pointed to me and said, "This woman needs a place to stay for the night and some help getting back on her feet. I know you can help her."

The receptionist started to speak but Angel cut her off.

"I think we might be able to help her. I know we are full right now, but I have an air mattress in my office she can sleep on tonight until we can find something else in the morning. Will that be okay?"

As she asked the question, she looked at me.

I nodded and said, "Yes, anything you can do will be fine. I really appreciate it because I have no other place to go."

The receptionist just looked at me with a scowl on her face. I wanted to lick my tongue out at her, but I was too grateful that someone was finally giving me a break.

I thanked the police officers for their help and followed Angel through the door behind the receptionist's desk. She walked me down a hallway that had several other doors. When we got to the end of the hallway, she led me into an office. She rearranged some boxes to make room for my bags, then she asked me to sit in one of the chairs next to her desk.

Angel pulled out several pieces of paper and started to tell me about the shelter and the services they provided.

"It's late now and I know you are tired. You will stay in this room tonight. Tomorrow, we will find you another room with a real bed and you will meet with one of our case workers. Are you hungry?"

When I nodded, Angel led me down another long hallway that led to the kitchen. She went to the refrigerator and pulled out a few containers. I watched as she assembled a sandwich. Then she pulled out an apple, a banana, and a bottle of water from the refrigerator.

As I ate, she told me that the shelter would be able to help me get back on my feet.

The next morning, Angel introduced me to Mrs. Justice, the shelter's social worker. As soon as I shook Mrs. Justice's hand, I had a strong sense of déjà vu. It was as if I had seen her somewhere before. I didn't have much time to search my mind through because Mrs. Justice immediately got to work helping me to get set up with housing assistance and job interviews.

After a long hard nine months, I felt as if things were finally turning back around in the right direction. God had finally answered my prayers.

Many people face challenges throughout their lives that may lead them to lose their home, eventually becoming homeless. Homelessness is not a choice and there are many reasons why people experience homelessness, including the lack of structural supports for those experiencing poverty, job loss, and inadequate discharge planning for those leaving hospitals, correctional facilities, and mental health facilities. Homeless is a problem we all could face; this means it can happen to anybody.

www.hud.gov • www.va.gov

CHAPTER 13
Pouring My Heart Out

· · · · · · · · · · · ·

The psychiatrist Mrs. Justice referred me to had an office a few blocks away from the women's shelter. I walked down the street very slowly; I was not looking forward to having to open my heart up to a stranger. Suddenly, the sky opened up, and it seemed as if buckets of water were being poured down.

I ducked under the awning of a building to get out of the rain and searched my bag for something to cover my head. I didn't have an umbrella, but there was a shower cap at the bottom of my bag.

This is better than nothing, I thought as I tucked my hair under the shower cap and continued my trip to the psychiatrist's office. By the time I arrived, my clothes were soaked, and I was in an even worse mood than I had been when I left the women's shelter.

The receptionist greeted me with a scowl. Apparently, I did not look as if I belonged in their office. As I approached the desk, he looked me up and down. His frown grew more profound when he noticed the shower cap on my head.

"It can't be raining that hard outside," he said with a snarky attitude.

My patience was hanging on by a tiny thread. Not only did I

not want to come to this appointment in the first place, but I was soaking wet. I took a few deep breaths to calm myself; it would not be in my best interests to give in to my urge to cuss this man out.

"It is raining very hard out there," I responded as calmly as I could.

I guess he saw the *don't mess with me* look on my face because he didn't say another word about the weather or my appearance. Handing me a clipboard and a few forms, he pointed to the waiting area.

"Please complete these forms and bring them back to me when you are done."

I took the forms and sat as far away as I could from the receptionist's desk. It didn't take long for me to fill out the forms. The information was pretty standard. A few moments after I handed the paperwork back to the receptionist, my name was being called.

I looked up to see a woman wearing a grey pants suit. She had a huge smile on her face and her eyes were welcoming.

"Hi, I'm Dr. Paradise. Come with me."

I followed Dr. Paradise down a short hall and into a medium-sized office. One side of the room looked like a standard office with a desk, two chairs, and a filing cabinet. The other side looked like a living room with a sofa, a high-backed chair, and a coffee table. An oriental area rug sat underneath the coffee table, and there was a tall lamp standing next to the sofa.

Dr. Paradise pointed to the sofa and asked me to have a seat. She sat across from me in the high-backed chair. As soon as I sat down, I heard a knock on the door. When Dr. Paradise invited the person in, I saw a young woman who looked to be in her early twenties holding a notebook.

"This is Newbie. She is a master's psychology student and is interning with me this semester. Do you mind if she sits in on our session?"

I looked at Newbie and shrugged. "Sure. She can sit in," I said.

She pulled one of the desk chairs closer to us and sat down with her legs crossed. She looked just as nervous as I felt.

The three of us sat in silence for a moment. Looking at the floor and taking deep breaths, I tried to calm my nerves before the session began. After a few more moments of the long silence, I started to feel a bit awkward. I noticed Newbie and Dr. Paradise looking at me in a strange manner.

Did they expect me to start this thing off?

This was my first session with a psychiatrist, and I had no idea what to expect. A few moments passed, then I realized they were looking at my head. I still had on the shower cap. The reception-ist had thrown me in such a tizzy that I forgot to take it off.

Oh well, it is what it is. I decided to keep it on. After all, they probably already thought I was crazy. This would be just one more thing they could write in their notes.

Realizing I was not going to take the shower cap off, Dr. Paradise cleared her throat and said, "Strong, since this is your first appointment, I would like to tell you a little about policies and how our therapy works."

Dr. Paradise gave me all of the rules and regulations of the sessions. She told me about the privacy policy and how her office would maintain my records. Then, she let me know that I could share anything in the sessions because everything I shared would be kept confidential.

"Whatever you say in this office, stays in this office," she said.

I nodded my head and thanked her. I had never been comfortable with sharing any of my personal business with others. This was going to be a very hard thing for me to do. Knowing that she would not share what I said with others was important to me.

"Do you have any questions?" Dr. Paradise asked.

"No, I understand everything you said."

"Great...Now, I know you are feeling anxious about seeing me today, Strong. It is a common feeling, but don't let your fears interfere with you getting the help and treatment that you need."

She paused and looked at me to make sure I was following along. I nodded my head in response and she continued,

"I want you to know that it is okay to cry, feel awkward, or experience various kinds of emotions while discussing your concerns. I know that being open and sharing your story will take a lot of strength and courage, which can feel emotionally exhausting, especially if you've suppressed your emotions for quite a long time. I also know that some of the questions that I will be asking you about your history may bring up sensitive issues, such as a history of trauma or abuse. If you don't feel comfortable or ready to share, please let me know that you're not ready to discuss the issue in further detail."

After making her spiel, Dr. Paradise started asking me questions.

"Have you ever been diagnosed with a mental illness?"

"No."

"What about anyone in your family?"

"No, not that I know of."

"Ok. What about anxiety? Have you ever experienced anxiety?"

I thought about that question for a moment and decided to answer truthfully.

"Yes, I feel tense, nervous, and I am unable to relax. I worry a lot and I often think about bad experiences; it's like I am on pins and needles all the time."

Dr. Paradise nodded and wrote for a moment on her notepad. I could see Newbie was also taking copious notes.

"What about depression?" Dr. Paradise asked. "Have you ever had feelings of depression?"

"I don't know if it's depression, but I constantly feel sad, I feel down and I cry frequently when I think about something that happened in my past. I've also had a lot of stressful life events happen to me lately. Getting through the day is very overwhelming. It is like living in a black hole."

"You mentioned something that happened in your past. Was this in your childhood?" Dr. Paradise asked.

"No. I had a good childhood. I can only remember one negative event and it wasn't from anyone in my family."

"What happened?"

"It was when my fifth-grade teacher. Ms. Apple yelled at me and told me that I would never graduate from high school, I would never be anyone important, and that I would never succeed in life. I think she was mad because one of my classmates and I were talking too much in class. It upset me really bad, but my Mom told me not to worry about what Ms. Apple had said. My mother also told me when people tell you that you can't do a certain thing, just show them, better than you can tell them. After I graduated from high school, my best friend and I saw Ms. Apple at the State Fair and I went up to her and let her know that what she told me in fifth grade was wrong."

"Good for you," Dr. Paradise said.

She looked at her notes for a few moments and then asked, "Do you ever feel disconnected from yourself?"

"Ummm…no. I don't feel disconnected from myself. It's other people. I feel disconnected from others, but not from myself."

"Ok…what about mood swings? Do you have any mood swings?

"Sometimes," I replied. "There are times when my mood swings are like a roller coaster. I get very irritable. It feels like I woke up on the wrong side of the bed."

"Tell me about your sleep habits. How do you sleep? Do you have nightmares or bad dreams?"

"Most nights, it's difficult for me to sleep. I toss and turn and wake up often during the night. I also have bad dreams most nights. If I do finally fall asleep, they wake me right back up."

Dr. Paradise stopped writing for a moment and asked, "Have you ever heard of PTSD—Post Traumatic Stress Disorder?"

"Yes, I've heard of it before."

"Do you find it hard to stop thinking about a very difficult event that has happened to you? When something happens that reminds you of the event, does that trigger a very large response in you? Do you find that you avoid things that remind you of the event?"

"Yes to all of the above." I said.

I could tell Dr. Paradise wanted me to say more, but I just sat there waiting for her next questions. I was going to be totally honest with her, but I was not going to give her more details than necessary at this point. I was still getting comfortable with her and even opening up this much was a strain on my emotions.

The room was silent for a moment, then Dr. Paradise continued with her questions.

"Have you ever thought about suicide?"

I shook my head vehemently. "No, suicide has never been an option for me."

That seemed to be the last question on her mental health checklist because she put the papers down for a moment and looked at me carefully.

"Why are you here, Strong?"

I took a deep breath and said, "I did not come here because I wanted to. Mrs. Justice at the women's shelter instructed me to come here for help. She thinks that I have serious issues that need to be addressed before I can move forward with my life."

"What do you think those issues are?" she asked.

"I think they are issues that started when I was in the military."

Dr. Paradise picked up the papers she had been looking over as she questioned me.

"I did not know you were in the military," she said as she made more notes.

"Yes. I served in the military for four years."

"Ok...what happened in the military to cause the issues you think you have?"

I sat quietly for a few moments. *Was I ready to open up to her about my traumatic experiences in the military?*

"Remember Strong, you can feel free to talk about anything and everything in this session. And, you only have to tell me what you are comfortable with. If it's too much right now, you can just give me the basic details."

I was grateful to Dr. Paradise for being so gentle with me. The truth about what happened had been locked away inside of me for so long. I wasn't sure I could even get the words out.

"Ummmm...Like I said, I was in the military for four years..."

As I told Dr. Paradise about the night Sergeant Cobra raped me and the imprisonment and torture that followed, my whole body trembled. As I told my story, I was aggressively stomping my feet on the floor in anger while I was sitting on the sofa. All of a sudden, my shoe flipped up in the air and hit Newbie in the head. Newbie stood up and immediately ran out of the office.

"Sorry about that," I said.

Wow, I didn't intend for my shoe to hit Newbie in the head; it just happened. I guess I scared poor Newbie. It felt as if I had been talking for hours. I was so exhausted and emotionally drained.

"Thank you for opening up to share part of your story with me, Strong. I can tell how difficult it is for you. I am glad you decided to trust me enough to start talking about it. Take a few deep breaths and tell me how you feel right now."

I took the deep breaths very slowly. As I breathed in and out, I felt my body calm down and my emotions became stable again.

"I honestly don't know how I feel. This is way too emotional for me. I had to revisit this painful memory and disclose embarrassing issues all over again; I will definitely have upsetting nightmares tonight. I've been holding this heavy burden inside of me for so long; I have been damaged and traumatized for years. And this is only the beginning."

This is only the beginning of my story; I didn't even get a chance to tell her about Empower and the rest of my major issues. She is going to be swept away when I do tell her. I don't want to talk about it anymore today; I just want to go home now.

"I know there is a lot more to your story. But we have done enough for today. The first session is always the hardest one. You did a great job. I am so glad you took the first step to get the help you need."

Dr. Paradise turned around in her chair and picked up a card off of her desk. After writing on the card, she handed it to me. My next appointment was set for a week later. Dr. Paradise told me to take it easy and gave me a breathing technique to use any time I felt anxious or overwhelmed.

I have to admit that when I walked into the office, I had an attitude. My mood was as gloomy as the weather outside. But the past hour with Dr. Paradise lifted my mood just a bit. I feel a lot better than I thought I would after talking about the things that happened to me. Maybe this therapy thing wouldn't be so bad.

CHAPTER 14
Lifting a Burden
· · · · · · · · · · · ·

"It's a beautiful day outside, Strong. Would you like to go for a walk?"

I had been coming to therapy sessions with Dr. Paradise for almost two months now; this was the first time she ever asked me this question.

I looked out of the window behind her desk and noticed the day was bright and sunny. It looked a whole lot more appealing outside than it did in this stuffy office.

"Yes, I would love to go for a walk," I said, jumping up from the sofa that had become my spot during our sessions.

Maybe while we were walking, Dr. Paradise wouldn't be able to ask me so many questions.

No such luck. As we walked, Dr. Paradise asked me questions as if we were in her office. The strange thing about it was that I answered her questions more freely. Being able to move in a wide-open space where I did not feel confined made me feel more relaxed. It certainly helped that Dr. Paradise was not looking at me as she usually did, with her notepad and pen in hand. This was just like a regular chat with a friend.

"Strong, how do you feel about the military?" Dr. Paradise asked.

This was a question she had asked me many times before, but I had always avoided responding. There was too much involved in answering that question and I had never been able to speak of the military without breaking down. Today, as we walked toward the lush green park adjacent to Dr. Paradise's office building, I finally answered the question.

"I think the military is a good thing. Even though a lot of bad things happened to me during my time in the military, I don't blame the entire system. I can see now how a few bad people can make everything seem worse."

Dr. Paradise smiled and nodded and asked me to continue.

"My original goal was to be in the military all of my career. I wanted to serve my country and really make a difference. I know if circumstances would have been different, I would have stayed in the military until I retired."

As I talked to Dr. Paradise about my hopes for my military career, I realized I wasn't as tense as I normally was when I discussed anything to do with the military. I was still sad and hurt by what happened to me, but I didn't feel the anger or rage that usually came whenever anyone brought up anything to do with the military.

Dr. Paradise was pleased with the progress I was making. I enjoyed our session outside. From that point on, whenever the weather was nice, I would request we walk during our sessions.

* * *

On the Thursday after Memorial Day, I entered Dr. Paradise's office and slammed myself onto her sofa. It was a nice day outside, but when she asked me if I wanted to go for a walk, I told her that I was not in the mood for walking.

"What's wrong? What happened?" Dr. Paradise asked with concern.

I had made so much progress since my early days of therapy when I would always come to the sessions with an attitude, so I know she must have been confused by my sudden relapse.

"I was assaulted again." I told her in anger.

"What? When? Where?" Dr. Paradise asked me.

I told Dr. Paradise about my trip to the grocery store on Memorial Day. I had gone to the store early in the morning so I would not be in a crowd later that day. I told her how as I was walking down one of the aisles, a man approached me. He looked like a nice and respectable older man so I didn't feel nervous with him being in the aisle with me. When he got close to me, I backed up a bit, trying to let him pass. I told her how he got very close to me and said, "You are a pretty little thing."

Then he groped me.

"What did you do? Did you tell the store security?" Dr. Paradise asked.

"No, I just ran out of the store."

"Why didn't you tell anyone?"

"What? The first time someone assaulted me, I was beaten and thrown in jail so I wouldn't tell on them. The next time someone assaulted me, I was fired and lost everything because I told. I was not about to tell anyone anything!" I exploded.

I slumped over and put my head between my knees. I was feeling dizzy and starting to hyperventilate.

"Why does this keep happening to me?" I asked, trying to calm my breathing.

Dr. Paradise didn't answer. I think she was wondering the same thing.

When she finally spoke, she said, "Have you ever thought about taking self-defense classes?"

When I just shook my head, she continued, "There is a class that starts in a few weeks. I think you should sign up. Being able to defend yourself will give you a greater sense of power if something like this should happen again."

* * *

My first self-defense class was on a Tuesday night. The class was held at a community center near Dr. Paradise's office building. There were twelve ladies in the class; but almost half of them had taken the class before. Ninja, the instructor, was a feisty woman who liked to flirt. When I first entered the class, she winked at me and gave me a big smile. I didn't let that bother me. As long as she didn't get too close to me, everything would be just fine.

Before we started, Ninja had two ladies who had previously taken her class stand at the front of the room and talk about their experience. One of the ladies was very arrogant as she talked about how she was a black belt and very dangerous. I just rolled my eyes.

Why is she even here if she is so bad ass? I wondered.

The first few weeks of class went well. We learned various moves and stances that would help us if we felt threatened or were under attack. For the third class, Ninja had us pair up so that we could practice some of the moves. I wanted to be paired with Bambi, another first timer, because she was nice and didn't talk a lot.

Unfortunately, my partner was Ms. Black Belt. She swaggered over to me as if she was in charge. Even though the instructor had already told us exactly what to do, Ms. Black Belt felt the need to tell me again, as if I was slow. I just looked at her and wanted the class to be over.

I turned around to get some water before we started practicing. All of a sudden, Ms. Black Belt grabbed me from behind. Startled, I slammed her to the ground and started punching and kicking her. I heard people moving around, but I couldn't make out what they were saying. It was as if her touch triggered something inside of me and all I could think was, *I am not going to let anyone assault me again.*

By the time the instructor was able to get me off of Ms. Black Belt, I had calmed a bit. I realized where I was and allowed her to take me to the other side of the room. Ms. Black Belt's face was bleeding and she was lying on the floor looking very scared.

I ran out of class and went home. I couldn't believe I had snapped like that. The next day, I called Ninja to find out if Ms. Black Belt was okay. I didn't like her, but I didn't want her to be hurt either.

"She is okay. Nothing too bad," Ninja said.

"I'm glad. I am so sorry that happened."

"I understand your reaction. The next time you come to class, we can talk about how to handle situations like that when someone approaches you from behind."

"I'm not coming back to class," I told her. "I don't want to hurt anyone else."

Ninja continued to reassure me that everything would be okay and that I should come back to class. I told her I would think about it.

At my next session with Dr. Paradise, she asked me how the self-defense class was going. I told her about my incident with Ms. Black Belt and she said the same thing Ninja said.

"Strong, you had a reaction that was triggered by what happened to you. I think you should continue to go to class so you can learn how to handle those types of situations."

I told her I would think about it, but I had no intention of going back to self-defense class.

Dr. Paradise let that subject go and moved on to another sensitive topic.

"Over the years, how have you been coping with this painful and hurtful burden for so long without reaching out for help?" Dr. Paradise asked me.

"I have been miserably dealing with it all by myself. I don't know why, and I don't know how I am still holding on. I just go to church and pray about it. I was taught to turn all of my problems over to the Lord, so that's what I do. Maybe God is trying to tell me something," I responded.

"In addition to the self-defense classes, I want you to start attending group sessions. It will be good for you to be around others who are experiencing some of the same things you are experiencing so you can see you are not alone in this," Dr. Paradise advised.

Dr. Paradise had recommended group sessions many times before. I had always rejected the idea because it was hard enough opening up to Dr. Paradise one on one. I didn't think I would be able to talk in front of a whole group of people looking at me.

"I think this group will really help you, Strong," Dr. Paradise said, handing me a pamphlet.

I looked at the pamphlet and read the details about the group sessions. I decided I would at least give it a try.

Dr. Paradise was so excited. "The next session is in two days. I know you are really going to enjoy it!" she exclaimed.

* * *

When I walked into the classroom for my first group session, I was a bit nervous. The room was full of people, and they were all standing around talking. I didn't know anyone in the room so I took a seat in the back near the door, just in case I wanted to leave early.

This group session was definitely not what I expected. I thought we would be sitting in a circle looking at each other talking about our feelings. Instead, the room was set up with tables and chairs in a classroom style. There were two instructors, one man and one woman. The woman was short and petite, while the man looked like he should be playing on a professional basketball team.

The instructors talked and gave people in the group a chance to ask questions or share their own experiences, but there was no pressure for me to speak. This was more about learning than it was about trying to get me to spill out all of my feelings.

Each week, there was a different topic for the group. We learned about how to control our emotions and manage our feelings. We learned about how we could remain calm in tense situations. We also learned how to manage our anger and stop before we said or did anything that could harm others or ourselves. The techniques and tips the instructors gave us were very helpful. I can even admit, I enjoyed hearing about how the other people in the class were using the tips in their own lives.

Noticing that some people talked more than others, the instructors started assigning people to share at each class. Two people were assigned for each session and they would talk about something that happened to them over the past few weeks that made them angry or feel out of control and talk about it in front of the group.

I did not want to participate. I was just starting to like this class and now they wanted me to talk? When it was my turn, I stood in front of the room with my knees shaking. I told the group about my experience a few weeks before when a driver cut me off and almost hit my car. I told them how he had rolled down his window and called me names and how I retaliated by throwing some coins I had in my cup holder at his car.

The instructors and the entire group just listened to me. They didn't judge me or laugh at me. Instead of criticizing me, the instructors just asked, "What did you learn from that experience?"

"I was very lucky," I said. "The guy could have followed me home and really hurt me. Or I could have caused an accident."

When I sat back in my seat, I was relieved. Sharing had not been so bad. I was afraid that they would criticize me or tell me I did something wrong. Instead, they helped me learn a real lesson.

Shortly after I arrived home that evening, my doorbell started ringing. It was my neighbor, holding a large box.

When I opened the door, he said, "This package came to my place by mistake. It's yours."

I looked at the box and noticed that it had already been opened.

"This is my package?" I asked him. "If it's my package, why did you open it?"

"Look, I didn't know it was yours at first. Then, I saw it wasn't mine and wondered why it was on my door. It could have been a bomb or something."

"What?" I looked at the guy in confusion.

A bomb? Is this guy crazy? I can't believe he opened my package. I should cuss him out.

I started to open my mouth and then closed it. I thought about the class I had just attended and all the things I had learned about controlling my anger. I took a deep breath and counted to ten.

"Thank you," I said, taking the package and closing the door.

The next time I was in the group session, I raised my hand to speak. The instructor looked surprised because I had never volunteered to speak before. When he asked me what I wanted to share, I told the group about my experience with my neighbor. Everyone clapped and cheered after I told them how I responded to the guy in a calm manner.

I couldn't wait to tell Dr. Paradise about it all during our next session. She was proud of me and congratulated me on my growth during the class.

* * *

At first, I felt a bit uneasy because I was experiencing something new; it was overwhelming and emotionally challenging to confront specific topics and realities. I revealed painful emotions, embarrassing and shameful feelings, and troubling memories during my therapy sessions. Though it was scary at first, I now have established a good rapport with Dr. Paradise; she is the one person I can be totally honest with, without any fear of judgment. My only regret throughout the whole experience is that I didn't do it sooner. I really wish I'd sought help earlier to avoid so many meltdowns. Taking the first step to seek help has changed my life. I know that I still have a long way to go, but I am a survivor, and I will get through this because I am **Strong.**

Post Traumatic Stress Disorder (PTSD) is a mental health condition that's triggered by a terrifying event — either experiencing it or witnessing it. PTSD is a lasting consequence of traumatic ordeals that cause intense fear, helplessness, or horror, such as a sexual or physical assault, the unexpected death of a loved one, an accident, war, or natural disaster. Most people who go through traumatic events may have temporary difficulty adjusting and coping.

PTSD symptoms may include

- flashbacks
- nightmares
- and severe anxiety
- as well as uncontrollable thoughts about the event

PTSD symptoms usually start within one month of a traumatic event, but sometimes symptoms may not appear until years after the event. These symptoms cause significant problems in social or work situations and in relationships. They can also interfere with your ability to go about your normal daily tasks.

www.mentalhealth.va.gov

CHAPTER 15
Keeping the Faith
. . . .

The Bible says, "Train up a child in the way he should go, and when he is old, he will not depart from it."

My life and journey have proved that to be true.

When I was growing up, my mother and grandmother took my siblings and me to church every Sunday. As a young child, I would walk into the church behind my grandmother, strutting in her Sunday's best. She wore colorful hats, prim and proper gloves, the fanciest of dresses and suits, and she had the attitude to match. My grandmother was always in fashion, but it wasn't in a stuck-up kind of way. She wanted to present the best she had to God, and she made sure that everyone else in her family looked their best as well.

When my sisters and I got older and started to go out on Saturday nights, we tried to stay home on Sunday mornings to recuperate. But my mother and grandmother were not having it. My mother would always say: "You found something to wear last night to go to the night clubs, so you will find something to wear on Sunday morning to go to church."

Although I was baptized at the age of 12 and spent every Sunday in church and Sunday school with my family, I was not so diligent after leaving home.

The years of strain and heartache took me to a place where I was barely attending worship services each week. It got to the point where I was only attending church on Easter Sunday. Not that I didn't believe in God, but I just didn't go to church anymore.

But church and God were still in me. At the very lowest point of my life, after surviving assault and homelessness, I knew deep inside that I had to turn back to God.

I can remember an incredibly vivid moment right before I lost my home, crying out to God in torment and despair. I asked Him to help me through my situation and to turn things around. I fell asleep with the television on, and I awoke to the sound of a man's voice.

Confused, I sat up and looked around my room, trying to see who was in there with me. When I realized the voice was coming from the television screen, I reached for the remote control to turn it off, but the man's words stopped me. He was speaking about letting the past go and moving into what God has for us. His words were so uplifting and encouraging.

The man was Joel Osteen, and his words shifted something inside of me. I started to remember the lessons I learned in church on Sundays with my mother and grandmother. I started to feel better.

After that night, I started to tune in to watch Joel Osteen whenever he was broadcasting.

In one particular message, he said,

"In this life, God warns that we will have trials and tribulations. The good news is that He also promises to deliver us from them all! Now, He doesn't necessarily say that He will deliver us instantly, or the way we expect, or on our schedule. It can be tempting to get discouraged when things don't happen the way you expect. But when you feel like trouble is surrounding you, that's when you have to dig your heels in and say, "I'm not giving up because God promised me victory!" If you are going through a dark time today, keep moving through it! Remember, it's always darkest just before the dawn appears. That difficulty didn't come to stay, it came to pass. Your job is to stay in faith and keep praising and thanking Him for delivering you. Set your hope in Him, stir up your faith, and keep believing because soon you will see the victory God has prepared for you! Hard times may have held you down, but they will not last forever. When all is said and done, you will be better off than before.

Those words spoke to my heart. I felt as if I was at rock bottom. I had no idea that there were even more trials and tribulations to come. God had allowed me to hear those words because He knew I would need them.

Even after I lost my home and found myself sleeping on a park bench, Joel Osteen's words continued to play in the back of my mind. I think that's why I never fully lost my mind. I had some very rough times, but I knew God was with me in the midst of it all. There was always a part of me that knew things would turn around.

After finding the shelter and getting the support I needed to get back on my feet with a job and permanent housing, I decided it was time to start going back to church.

Unfortunately, the church I had gone to before was closed. I couldn't turn to them and felt lost.

One day while I was in the computer room at the public library, a lady sat down at the computer right next to mine. She said hello to me in a cheerful tone, and she looked like she wanted to start a conversation.

I said hello and quickly put my head back down. I am not sure why she sat right next to me. There were other computers on the other side of the room that weren't being used.

Seeing that I did not want to talk, the friendly lady turned her attention to the young girl sitting on the other side of her.

The girl had her head down, and she was crying silently. The happy lady consoled the girl and told her that everything would be okay. She invited the girl to attend her church. At the word church, my ears perked up. I intently listened to the conversation. When the lady took a breath, I asked her to tell me more about her church. She told me where the church was located and the service times.

The very next Sunday, I attended the church and was immediately drawn in. Everyone was engaging. The pastor preached the word of God. I attended that church for a very long time, but I never saw the lady who invited me. It is true that God will send you what you need at just the right time. Just like He sent me the message from Joel Osteen when I was at a very low point, He sent the woman in the library to nudge me in the right direction when He knew I needed support from a local church.

Church has been a life-changer for me. I am a true witness that prayer changes things. I **know by** keeping the faith and walking the faith, the Lord will be with me every step of the way. This is God's plan. Maybe one of these days, I will give my own testimony about my painful and troubled life, how the Lord showed up in my life with such grace, how the Lord worked a miracle through me, and how I overcame so many obstacles because I am God's Masterpiece. I am **Strong**, I am Blessed, and I am Highly Favored.

Unity Prayer Line	Need A Prayer
1-800-669-7729	**1-303-256-2899**

CHAPTER 16
The Truth Comes To The Light
. . . .

"Hey, mom. I want to talk to you about something."

The tone of Empower's voice let me know he wanted to have a serious conversation. Had something terrible happened?

Empower is doing so well. He rose quickly through the military ranks and became a highly decorated officer. He is a loving husband and father to four beautiful children. With everything going so well in his life, I thought it was best for me not to tell him about losing my job, my home, and everything else. There are just some things you don't tell your children. After all, I am his mother. I am supposed to take care of him. He is not supposed to take care of me.

Had he somehow found out about what was going on in my life?

"What do you want to talk about, son?" I asked him nervously.

Empower let out a long sigh and finally said, "I want to talk to you about my father. I know where he is, and I want to see him."

All of the breath left my body. I was so glad I was already sitting down. Otherwise, I might have passed out. I was expecting him to want to talk about something serious, but never in my wildest dreams would I ever think he would want to talk about his father.

When Empower was growing up, he would often ask me about his father—who he was and where he was. Every time he asked, I would avoid his questions and change the subject. Finally, when he turned sixteen, I told him the truth about his father and what happened between us. That conversation didn't go over so well. Empower became very angry and said he hated his father. He said he wished he had never asked about him. After that day, Empower never spoke to me about his father again.

Now he was telling me that he had found his father.

"How?" I asked, trying to maintain my composure. "How did you find your father?"

"I took one of those DNA tests that help you determine your heritage and ancestry. I knew my father's last name and that he was in the military, so I put that into the database. Then, some people contacted me through Facebook. It turns out they are my siblings, and we have been chatting. I want to meet my father and I want you to go with me."

What?

I was still trying to process the fact that Empower had found his father. I couldn't even begin to comprehend the fact that he actually wanted to meet him and for me to go too.

"I don't think that is such a good idea. I do not want to see him ever again." I told Empower.

"Mom, I need you to go with me. Plus, I think it would be good to show him how well you are doing now even with all he put you through."

Empower thought I was doing so well. He had no idea.

"Mom, I also think it's time for me to meet your family too."

Where was all of this coming from? Empower knew I had brothers and sisters and a family back in Buffalo, but I had never told them about Empower. I talked to them occasionally, but we were not as close as we were before my mother died. They didn't know anything about what was happening in my life.

"Son, where is all of this coming from?"

"I just think it's time. I know it was just you and me growing up, but I did the DNA test because I wanted to know more about where I came from. You've been a great mom to me, but I know we have more family. I want to get to know them, and I want my children to get to know them too."

There was nothing I could say to that. I knew Empower was right. I had kept him away from my family for his entire life; it was way past time for him to get to know them. And I guess he was right about his father too.

"Okay, son. I will go with you to meet your father and take you to see our family in Buffalo."

*** *

Empower and I flew across the country to the East Coast. He found out his father lived in New Jersey, which wasn't too far from Buffalo, New York.

On our drive from the airport, I had to give myself several pep talks. Just the thought of seeing Sergeant Cobra again made me feel anxious and brought up flashbacks of the last time I saw him. Next to me, Empower looked calm and poised. He was wearing his full military uniform with his rank and several medals on full display. I was so proud of the man he had grown to be and as I looked at my son, my nerves settled a bit.

We parked in front of a massive house. It had to be at least a six-bedroom home with a large front and back yard. There must have been at least a couple of acres of land surrounding the home.

How could he be living in a mansion when I could barely make it in my government-subsidized one bedroom apartment? While I was struggling, he was living in the lap of luxury. Life just wasn't' fair.

Empower rang the doorbell, and we could hear footsteps approaching.

"Who is it?" a strong male voice asked.

I got chills because, after all these years, I still recognized that voice.

"I am Captain Empower. I am looking for Kingston Cobra."

Kingston Cobra?

After all of this time, I finally knew Sergeant Cobra's first name.

The door opened immediately, and there was a huge smile on Sergeant Cobra's face. He looked at Empower standing in front of him; all decked out in his full military regalia. I guess he thought Empower had come to talk to him about the military days or give him some kind of award. Sergeant Cobra extended his hand to greet Empower, then he noticed me. His hand dropped and his smile immediately faded into a look of shock.

"What is this all about?" Sergeant Cobra asked. His tone was gruff and suspicious.

Empower cleared his throat and said, "My name is Captain Empower and I am your son."

Sergeant Cobra did a double-take and looked between me and Empower several times. I could tell the moment when he realized the truth of Empower's statement. His eyes clouded over with something that looked like regret and his jaw tensed.

Instead of welcoming us in, Sergeant Cobra stepped outside and closed the door behind him. There was probably someone in the house he didn't want to hear our conversation.

"Let's go to the garden to talk." Sergeant Cobra said.

We followed him to the back of the house where there was a garden with several kinds of flowers. The garden was circle shaped with a bench and two chairs. Empower sat on the bench and Sergeant Cobra sat on one of the chairs. I just stood there. There was too much nervous energy built up inside of me to sit down.

Empower explained to his father how he had taken a DNA test and signed up for the genealogy and family history service that had connected him to his siblings. The entire time Empower was talking, Sergeant Cobra looked as if he was about to pass out. Maybe he was remembering how Empower was conceived. I know I certainly was.

As I paced back and forth around the garden, all I could think about was the fact that I was once again in the presence of the man who had raped me. It was a very traumatic experience, and I didn't know how much more of this I could take. I was trying the breathing exercises Dr. Paradise taught me and I was using all of the anger management skills I picked up during my group sessions to keep my emotions under control.

Empower and his father talked for several minutes, then Sergeant Cobra came over to where I was pacing.

"Strong, why didn't you tell me I have a son?"

My head snapped up. I had rage in my eyes.

"Why didn't I tell you about Empower? Are you kidding me? You raped me. I got pregnant because you raped me. We were not in some kind of relationship. You raped me and then had me thrown in jail so I wouldn't tell anyone what you had done. You told me you would kill me if I told anyone. And now you are asking me why I didn't tell you about my son?"

I was screaming by this point, and all of the pent-up emotions I had been trying so hard to hold in spilled out.

I could not believe he was standing there talking to me as if we had been a couple or something. This man was out of his mind.

Empower wrapped his arms around me and led me back to the car. As I climbed into the passenger's seat, I looked up and saw a woman standing in the window. I wonder if she was his wife. What kind of lies would he tell her about why we came to see him? I did not care what he told her. I would never speak to him again.

Our next stop on this trip down memory lane was to see my family in Buffalo.

My emotions were raw, and I didn't know if I would be able to make it through another blast from my past.

As we drove, Empower told me about the conversation he had with his father. They had exchanged telephone numbers and agreed to keep in touch. I didn't know how to take that piece of information. I felt conflicted because I hated Sergeant Cobra, but I didn't want Empower to have that kind of hate in his heart.

* * *

When we arrived at my family home in Buffalo, the emotions started swirling again. We were going to the house I grew up in. My brother, Zazzle, lived there now with his family. I had not been to this house since my mother passed.

As we walked up to the door, I wiped tears from my eyes. The memories of being back home were overwhelming.

I could hear music playing and could smell food cooking. From the looks of the cars in the driveway and lined up on the street, we were about to walk into a full house.

"Maybe we should come back later. It looks like they are having a party or something." I said, hoping to convince Empower to turn around and go back to the car.

Empower was not hearing it. He just grabbed my hand and led me to the front door.

My brother opened the door, and his face broke out into a huge grin when he saw me. He picked me up and twirled me around.

"Strong! Baby Sis, I am so happy to see you. It's been a long time."

I knew my brother loved me, but I wasn't expecting a reception like this.

Zazzle looked at Empower and asked, "Who's this?"

"This is Empower, my son," I told him.

Zazzle didn't hesitate to give Empower a big hug. He didn't ask me any questions; he just welcomed us into the house and shouted, "Hey, y'all! Look who's here!"

The house was filled with my family members. It was Zazzle's birthday, and they had all come to celebrate. Everyone gave us hugs and welcomed us without any questions. Well, everyone except my sister, Pyramid.

"Why is this the first time we are hearing that you have a son? He's a grown man, and you kept him a secret all this time?" Pyramid asked with an attitude.

I knew she would be the one who would start some mess.

"Look, I had my reasons," I told her. "Please don't' start causing trouble now."

Fortunately, Pyramid backed off. Maybe she could tell I wasn't up for answering a whole lot of questions. Of course, Pyramid and I have different opinions about certain things, but she is a woman of integrity, and she has great wisdom.

Empower seemed to be in seventh heaven. He laughed and joked with his cousins; he played cards with his uncles. It was as if they had known him all of his life.

I called Vegas and told her that Empower and I were in Buffalo. We had kept in touch over the years, but this is the first time I've seen her since I went to the West Coast. She came into the house and ran straight to me. When she saw Empower, she had tears in her eyes. Vegas was the only one who knew about Empower. She was happy to see him all grown up.

The visit to see my family was just what I needed after my encounter with Sergeant Cobra. It felt as if a huge weight had been lifted from my shoulders.

CHAPTER 17
Dilemma

· · · · · · · · · · · ·

After my family reunion in Buffalo, I felt better than I had in a long time. I was still trying to get my life back together, but I had new energy and hope that things would turn around soon.

I looked around my tiny apartment. It was a long way from the beautiful home I once had, but it was also very far away from the streets. I was so grateful for the Women's Shelter and all the help they had given me to help me get back on my feet.

I had a job, an apartment, and a car—even though it was so raggedy I held my breath when I put the key in the ignition, praying it would start.

As I looked around my apartment with gratitude, I noticed a big bag in the corner. It was one of the bags I had stuffed all of my important papers in when I had to move out of my house quickly. Deciding to get organized, I sat down at the kitchen table and started arranging the papers. The papers on the top of the pile were the ones I received on my first visit to the Women's Shelter. Mrs. Justice's card was there, and my intake paperwork with her signature. I remembered my first time meeting Mrs. Justice at the shelter and the feeling I had that I knew her from somewhere.

As I continued to sort through the papers, I came across some of my military paperwork. I tensed up when I saw the form the military had given me after my time in the Stockade Confinement Facility. At the bottom of the letter was a signature—Iowa Sway.

I looked at the signature on the letter. Then I riffled through my stacks of papers to find the intake paperwork from the Women's Shelter. The signatures on the documents were the same. And the names were the same. Except now, Iowa Sway was Iowa Sway-Justice.

I couldn't believe what I was seeing. Mrs. Justice was the Captain that had put me in the Stockade Confinement Facility. She was the one who was having an affair with Sergeant Cobra and locked me up just because he told her I was trouble.

I had to talk to her. I had an appointment with her for the next week, but I could not wait until then.

I jumped into my raggedy car and prayed that it would start. I drove the short distance to the Women's Shelter and hopped out.

It was late, but the Women's Shelter was still open. I parked my car behind the shelter and grabbed my pepper spray. The shelter was not in the best neighborhood, and sometimes some creepy people lurked around.

When I walked into the lobby area, I told the receptionist I wanted to see Mrs. Justice. She told me that she had just left and that I should come back tomorrow.

That was not what I wanted to hear. I stomped my foot and walked out of the building. I didn't know how I was going to be able to sleep with all the thoughts that were swirling around in my head.

As I approached my car at the back of the building, I heard a woman screaming, "Leave me alone!"

I looked up and saw a big man hit the woman. I started to walk away but knew that I couldn't let someone get hurt like this. I picked up a metal stick lying on the ground next to my car and walked toward the man.

His back was turned to me, so he didn't' see me when I hit him over the head with the stick. He fell to the ground. Blood poured from his head. I hoped he wasn't dead, but I was glad that he was not moving.

I reached my hand out to help the woman who he had been beating on, and I saw that it was Mrs. Justice.

My first thought was, I should have let him beat her up. *After all, she put me in jail, where I was beaten and traumatized for no good reason.*

But those thoughts quickly went away. As angry as I was at Mrs. Justice for the situation she put me in so many years ago, I would not wish that kind of thing even on my worst enemy.

I pulled out my phone and dialed 9-1-1. I am not sure what the dispatcher heard when I told her I needed help at the Women's Shelter, but ten minutes after my call, the fire truck, ambulance, and two police cars arrived on the scene.

The first person to approach us was a handsome fireman. He

asked me what happened and looked at me with interest as I gave my response. Mrs. Justice was still out of it, so the paramedics put her on a stretcher and started taking her to the ambulance.

As she was being wheeled away, she called out to me, "Strong, thank you so much for saving my life. What were you even doing here?"

I told her that I was glad I came when I did. I then told her that we needed to talk about something important but that it could wait until she felt better.

An officer came over to get my statement. I recognized Officer Lifesaver as one of the officers that had originally brought me to the Women's Shelter.

"Hey, you are a hero," he said with a big smile.

Officer Lifesaver told me how proud he was of me and how they needed more people like me in the community.

"I knew you were one of the good ones," he said.

Officer Lifesaver told me I could go home but asked if I would come down to the police station the next day to give a statement about what happened. The man I hit with the metal stick was still alive, but he had a really big gash in his head. Officer Lifesaver knew that I had acted in defense of Mrs. Justice, and he wanted to make sure there would be no repercussions for me after the incident.

I got in my car and told him I would come to the station in the morning. I started my car and said a silent prayer hoping my car wouldn't backfire. As I drove away, I saw Officer Lifesaver talking and laughing with the handsome fireman. Although they were talking to each other, the fireman's eyes were on me. He smiled and waved as I turned the corner.

The next day, I went to the police station and told Officer Lifesaver all about the incident. I told him how I had come out of the Women's Shelter and heard a woman screaming. It told him how I had hit the man over the head with the metal stick to get him off of the woman.

He wrote everything down and told me that he would be in touch if they needed any further information. As I was leaving, he handed me a business card.

"I already have your card," I told him.

"This isn't from me. It's Mr. Fireman's card. He is the firefighter from last night. He wanted me to give you his card and tell you to call him," Officer LifeSaver winked as I took the card.

***

It took me two weeks to call Mr. Fireman. I felt sparks when I saw him for the first time, but I wasn't sure if I was ready to start dating. I was still working out my problems and trying to get back on solid ground. Dating would just complicate things.

But I couldn't get Mr. Fireman out of my mind. I thought about him all the time and wondered if it could really work out with him. Finally, I decided to give him a call. When he answered the phone and I introduced myself, he was thrilled to hear from me. He told me that he was starting to think that I wasn't going to call. And I told him that I almost didn't.

Our first conversation lasted for hours. I found out his first name was Toronto and that he had been a fireman for twenty-eight years. He had two grown children who were the same age as Empower. I knew Officer Lifesaver had told him about my situation, but that didn't seem to matter to Toronto. We talked on the phone several more times before I agreed to go out on a date with him. He took me to a very nice, upscale restaurant and treated me like a queen.

"You knocked me off my feet from the moment I saw you. I think it was love at first sight for me," he told me as we ate the delicious meal.

His words gave me chills. I felt butterflies in my stomach. I had never had a man treat me so well before. I think I was falling for him too.

Our relationship blossomed into something very special. Toronto treated me with respect and always wanted to protect me. He was always a gentleman and made sure I was always taken care of. He did so many nice things for me—he even bought me a new car when my raggedy old one broke down.

I felt like Cinderella and Toronto was my Prince Charming. It seemed as if I was finally getting my happily ever after.

CHAPTER 18
Unfinished Business

· · · · · · · · · · · ·

After Mrs. Justice recovered from her attack, she called me for an appointment. She wanted to thank me for saving her life and to follow up with me on the matter I wanted to discuss with her.

When I walked into her office, Mrs. Justice hugged me tightly and babbled on and on about how grateful she was that I had come to the Women's Shelter that night. She rambled for about five minutes before she took a breath.

I was happy that I had been able to help her, but I wanted her to stop talking so that I could tell her what I wanted to say. I don't think she would be in such a good mood after that.

"Mrs. Justice, I have something important to talk to you about."

She sat back in her chair and smiled at me. "Okay, what do you want to talk about?"

I took in a deep breath and braced myself for the conversation.

"Were you ever in the military?" I asked her.

She nodded and smiled. "Yes, Strong. I was in the military. Quite a few years ago. Why do you ask?"

"I was in the military too," I told her.

I looked to see if she had a spark of recognition when I told her that, but she just kept smiling at me and nodding her head, waiting for me to continue.

"Did you know a man by the name of Sergeant Cobra?"

Mrs. Justice thought for a moment, and then she said, "Yes, I remember Sergeant Cobra. We served on the same base for a while."

I still didn't see any hint of recognition in Mrs. Justice's eyes. I guess she had really put her time in the military behind her. She seemed to really have no bad memories about that time. I wish I could say the same.

Mrs. Justice was still smiling at me, thinking we were about to reminisce about the good old days.

I pulled out a piece of paper from my bag and handed it to her. As she read it, she looked confused.

"What's this?" she asked.

"Mrs. Justice, you and Sergeant Cobra had me locked up in the Stockade Confinement Facility for an entire week for something I did not do. While I was in the facility, I was beaten and tortured. It was all done to keep me silent after Sergeant Cobra assaulted me."

Mrs. Justice's previously sunny disposition turned cloudy. She looked shocked and on the verge of tears. As I continued to tell her the entire story, Mrs. Justice shrank down in her chair and put her head in her hands. I could tell she was very upset about hearing this. I think she might need to have a session with Dr. Paradise after this conversation.

I finished telling her everything and we sat in silence for a long while. When she finally was able to look at me again, Mrs. Justice said, "I don't know what to say. I am so sorry that happened to you."

I was still enraged at what happened to me, but looking at Mrs. Justice's face, I knew that I couldn't hold a grudge against her any longer. Maybe she was just a pawn in Sergeant Cobra's game. Maybe she just went along with what he told her and never knew the whole story.

"I can't believe you knew all of this and still saved my life. What can I do for you?"

"Nothing," I said. "I don't want anything from you. I just wanted you to know what happened. This is why I have been so angry for all of these years. This is why I needed to see a therapist. I thank you for sending me to see Dr. Paradise. I have come a long way. I just hope that you will continue to help the women who come to this shelter."

CHAPTER 19
A Mind-Blowing Decision
· · · · · · · · · · · ·

"Hey, Strong. This is Premier. It's been so long since we've talked. I want to know how you are doing. Call me, please."

I listened to the voicemail message, but I did not immediately delete it as I had done with the many other ones Premier had left me over the past year.

She had been calling me on a regular basis, and every time she did, I ignored her. She reminded me too much of all the things that happened after my encounter with Edge. I know Premier was not a bad person and that she was the only one who I could really talk to at that company, but I just had not been able to face the betrayal and anger I felt toward everyone at that company.

Maybe it was the fact that I had confronted Sergeant Cobra and Mrs. Justice. Maybe it was my reconciliation with my family. Or maybe it was my growth after therapy and the group sessions. Whatever it was, I decided that I would finally speak to Premier.

I dialed her number. When she answered, I said, "Hi Premier, this is Strong. How are you doing?"

The shriek that came from the other end of the line was deafening. Premier was excited to hear from me, to say the least.

"Oh my gosh, Strong. Is this really you? I can't believe it."

Premier and I chatted for a while. She told me all about what was going on at the company and how everyone was upset when I was fired.

"I have been asking Golden about you, but he said he hasn't heard from you either."

I didn't respond to her. I just rolled my eyes. Golden hadn't heard from me because he never responded to my call the night after the Christmas Party. He didn't call me to ask me how I was after being fired. He just completely ghosted me and vanished into thin air.

I didn't tell Premier any of that, just like I didn't tell her about losing my house and becoming homeless. I let her carry the conversation. I chimed in here and there to answer a question or make a comment about something she said.

"My uncle's comedy club is having a big show in two weeks. I think you should come."

"I'll try," I said.

"Don't try. Come. I really want to see you."

I didn't make any promises to Premier about going to the comedy club. But, when I talked about it with Toronto, he said it would be a great date night.

On the night of the big show, Toronto and I arrived at the comedy club decked out as if we were walking the red carpet.

Toronto had bought me a new dress and told me he wanted the night to be exceptional.

Premier was standing near the entrance when Toronto and I walked in. She had a look of surprise and shock when she realized that Toronto was with me. She hugged me and told me that she had reserved a table for us in the front.

"I didn't know you were bringing a guest, but I think there is an extra seat at the table," she said.

When Toronto and I arrived at the table, there was already a man sitting there. I assumed it was Premier's date.

"Hi, we're friends of Premier. She told us to come to this table." I said.

The man turned around and greeted us. "Have a seat. There is plenty of room."

When the man looked at me, I almost fell over. It was Golden. No wonder Premier was so shocked to see Toronto with me. She probably set this whole thing up trying to get Golden and me back together.

I just smiled and introduced Golden and Toronto. Toronto knew about my time at the company and how I had been fired. I had also told him about Golden and how I had never heard from him again after the Christmas Party.

Toronto shook Golden's hand and said, "Hey, man. It's good to meet the man that let my beautiful lady get away."

Golden didn't say anything. He just sat there with a stupid look on his face.

The first half of the show was hilarious. Even with the tension at the table, Toronto and I had a great time. During the intermission, Toronto excused himself to go to the restroom.

"I'll be right back," he said as he kissed my cheek.

Golden had been staring at the two of us all night. When Toronto left the table, I asked him why.

"I miss you, Strong. We had something outstanding and I miss you."

"It's too late," I told him. "I'm finally happy after all I've been through."

Golden dropped his head and stared at the floor. I could tell he was feeling bad about the entire situation. I wish Premier would have never tried to set this up. It was awkward.

The MC hit the microphone a few times to get the attention of the crowd.

"Hey, y'all. We've got a few more minutes of intermission, but I have a special guest here who wants to say something."

I was digging around in my purse, not paying attention to what was happening on the stage, until I heard a familiar voice.

"Strong, can you come up here with me?"

My head popped up and I saw Toronto standing on the stage. What the heck? I was not about to get on that stage with him. I had no idea what was going on but I know I was not about to get up there in front of all of these people.

"Come on Strong," Toronto said.

The audience started chanting my name and I flushed with embarrassment.

I slowly walked to the stage and the MC helped me climb the steps. When I was standing next to Toronto, he pulled out a small box from his pocket and dropped to one knee.

"Strong, you are the most beautiful woman I have ever met. You are amazing and wonderful. I think I fell in love with you the moment I met you. These past months with you have been the best months of my life. I would be the luckiest man in the world if you would be my wife."

"Yes!" I told him.

This was the best night ever. I really love this man and he has been the best thing that has happened to me since I gave birth to Empower.

As we walked back to our table, everyone was cheering and congratulating us. When we got to our seats, I noticed Golden had left. I was glad because I didn't want anything ruining my special night.

We had a little more time before the show started again, so I hurried to the restroom before the lights went back out. As I was coming out, Golden was standing there.

"That should have been us," he said.

"No, it shouldn't have been us. You and I were not meant to be," I told him as I tried to walk past him.

"We were happy together. I just couldn't get over what happened with Edge. I can't believe you tried to seduce him."

"What?" I couldn't believe what I was hearing. "What did you say? I tried to seduce Edge? Are you serious?"

"Look, he told me what happened at the Christmas Party and I..."

"You what?" I interrupted. "You believed him?"

"Yes, he told me about how you tried to kiss him on the elevator and how you threatened to get him fired."

"You have it all wrong. That is not what happened at all. Edge assaulted me. When I told human resources about his attack, I was the one who was fired."

"I didn't know. I thought…"

I didn't let him finish. "Whatever you thought was wrong. And that is exactly why we were never meant to be."

I stormed away and walked back to the table.

When I got there, I told Toronto what Golden had said. He just gave me a big kiss and said, "You're mine now. He's just mad because he let you get away. Don't worry about it."

The rest of the show was just as good as the first half. Golden never came back to the table and that was just fine with me.

* * *

The week after the comedy show, Golden called and texted me several times a day.

He started out apologizing and pleading for me to give him another chance, telling me it was not too late for us. He told me he was sorry for believing Edge and not talking to me. He told me that he had never forgotten about me and he wanted me back.

Then, his begging and pleading turned into threats.

"Strong, I love you. I know you love me. We will be together. I won't let anything stand between us. I know your new man is a fireman and I can easily get to him. Remember, I was in the military and I know how to get rid of people. If he is gone, you will have to come back to me."

I listened to the message a few times then I blocked his number. I had no idea Golden was this crazy. I had certainly dodged a bullet all those months ago when he had stopped calling me.

A few days after I blocked Golden's number, I received a call from Premier. As soon as I answered, she started rambling so fast I could barely understand her.

"Slow down," I told her. "I can't understand what you are saying."

"It's Golden. I think he's going to do something terrible."

"Why? What happened?" I asked.

I had not told anyone about the phone calls Golden made nor about the messages he left. I had not taken his threats seriously. But now I was nervous.

"He just called me and asked me if I had talked to you. When I told him I hadn't he said you were ignoring him and that he wanted to get you back. He said it was all Edge's fault that you two broke up and he was going to make him pay. He said he knew Edge works late in the office on Thursdays and he was going there now to confront him."

Premier's words were flowing like a faucet and I could barely keep up with the conversation. All I knew was that Golden had snapped.

"We have to stop him," Premier said to me.

"Why do we have to stop him? I am not with Golden. I don't want to be in the middle of it."

"Strong, you can stop him."

I told Premier I would meet her at the office in twenty minutes. I told her she should call the police and tell them what she told me.

"I don't trust the police. I don't want Golden to go to jail."

When I arrived at the office, Premier met me in the parking lot and we entered the building using her key. We rode the elevator to the fourth floor and as soon as the doors opened, we could hear shouting.

The hallway was dark and the cubicles were empty. It was after hours so everyone had already left for the day. The only light we could see was coming from the end of the hallway where the executive offices were.

"You messed everything up! It's all your fault!"

We could hear Golden screaming as we raced down the hallway.

When we arrived at Edge's office, we saw Golden standing in front of Edge, shouting and waving a gun. Edge was sitting back in his chair with a look of terror on his face.

"Put the gun down, Golden. You don't want to do this," I said.

Golden turned around and the look on his face scared me. His eyes were filled with rage. I instantly regretted agreeing to come here and not calling the police.

"What are you doing here, Strong?" he asked, walking toward me.

"Premier called me and told me you were about to do something stupid. I do not want you to get hurt or hurt someone else. Please put the gun down and let Edge go."

"It was his fault we broke up. He told me his lies and I believed him. Now I am alone and miserable. You are with someone else and about to get married."

"You don't have to do this. You are a good man and you can find someone who loves you. But not if you do this. If you do this you will go to jail and your life really will be over."

I could see the rage leaving Golden's body. He put the gun on the desk and slumped to the floor in tears. As much as I didn't want Golden to go to jail, I knew we had to call someone to help him. He needed help.

Edge came around the desk and walked over to me.

"Thank you, Strong. I am so sorry for how things went down before. Even with all that I did to you, you still saved my life. You are a real hero."

I had no love for Edge and a few months ago, I probably would have let Golden shoot him. But my life was going too good for me to have something like that hanging over my head.

"I think you should call his daughter and tell her to come get him. Maybe she can take him to the hospital or something to get some help." I told Premier as I walked out of the office.

No matter how much pain you're experiencing right now, you're not alone. Many of us have had suicidal thoughts at some point in our lives. Feeling suicidal is not a character defect, and it doesn't mean that you are crazy, or weak, or flawed. It only means that you have more pain than you can cope with right now. But with time and support, you can overcome your problems and the pain and suicidal feelings will pass. Many kinds of emotional pain can lead to thoughts of suicide. The reasons for this pain are unique to each of us, and the ability to cope with the pain differs from person to person. We are all different. If you are experiencing negative thoughts, if you find yourself lost and you cannot see a way out, call a professional.

If you or someone you know has suicidal thoughts, get help right away through one or more of these resources:

- Reach out to a close friend or loved one.

- Contact a minister, a spiritual leader or someone in your faith community.

- **Call a suicide hotline number** — in the United States, call the National Suicide Prevention Lifeline at **1-800-273-TALK (1-800-273-8255)** to reach a trained counselor. Use that same number and press 1 to reach the Veterans Crisis Line.

- Make an appointment with your doctor or a mental health professional.

www.mentalhealth.va.gov

CHAPTER 20
You Reap What You Sow
· · · · · · · · · · · ·

As soon as I left the office building, I put Edge and Golden out of my mind. My life was going too good to let them mess it up. I was glad I could help Edge and I hoped Golden would get the help he needs, but I was not going to get wrapped up in their drama.

A few weeks later, Toronto and I attended the annual showdown between the Fire Department and the Police Department. It was a big event. All of the fire fighters, police officers, and their families came out to have fun and compete in various sports activities. The two biggest games were the men's football game and the women's basketball game. Toronto was playing on the Fire Department's men's football team. And, he had convinced me to play on the Fire Department's women's basketball team. It felt good to be a part of a couple and do these kinds of things together.

When the football game started, you would have thought I was a professional cheerleader the way I yelled and screamed for Toronto. He was playing wide receiver and he was one of the best players on the team. Officer Lifesaver was playing for the Police Department's team and he was pretty good, but he was no match for Toronto and the Fire Department. Every time Toronto caught the ball or scored a touchdown, he turned to make sure I saw him. I knew he was trying to show off for me and I loved it. I just keep cheering him on. Needless to say, the Fire Department won the game.

After the game, Toronto came over to the sidelines and gave me a big hug.

"Get your sweaty body off of me," I told him, laughing.

"You know you like it," he said, rubbing his sweaty face against my cheek.

He was right. I did like it.

He wrapped his arm around my shoulder, and we started walking towards the basketball court.

"How did I do out there?" he asked.

I just smiled at him and said, "I saw you trying to impress me out there. You did okay…"

"Okay? I scored three touchdowns. I think I did better than okay."

"So, what, you are just fishing for compliments?" I asked with a smirk.

Toronto laughed and said, "Yeah. I want you to tell me how good I was."

I just shook my head and laughed at him. Then, I said, "You were the best player on the team. You dominated the game. You are the only reason the Fire Department won. You carried the whole team…"

He put his hands up and stopped me.

"Now that's what I'm talking about. I am so glad you recognize my skill."

We both laughed and continued to walk to the basketball courts.

The women's basketball game was starting in a few moments and I was a little nervous. I was a great player when I was in the military, and I kept myself in great shape, but I had not played the game in a long time.

When we reached the basketball court, I saw Officer Good Deed stretching with the Police Department's team. I wonder if she would remember me from the night she and Officer Lifesaver found me sleeping on the park bench.

I walked over to the coach for the Fire Department's team and introduced myself.

"Hey, I'm Strong. I'm signed up to play on your team today."

He looked me up and down and said, "Are you any good?"

His abrasive question put me in defensive mode, and I said, "I'm the best player you will have on your team today."

"Oh really?" he said with a smirk. "We'll just have to see about that. What position do you play?"

"Point Guard," I responded.

"All right. Get warmed up and let's see what you're working with."

I walked over to the other women on the team and they greeted me much more warmly than the coach did. They smiled and shook my hand welcoming me to the team. We stretched for a few moments. Then the coach put us through a few warmup drills to get us ready for the game. By the time the game started, I was fired up. Games like this brought out my competitive side and I knew I would play my best so we could win.

Just like I had done for his game, Toronto was right on the sidelines cheering me on. The game was fast-paced and the women on both sides were very athletic. I pushed myself to compete. I blocked shots, played great defense, and I made some crucial assists. I also put up points in the double digits. The other team saw me as a threat and tried to foul me a lot. That just allowed me to score even more points when I went to the free throw line.

At the end of the game, I walked over to Toronto and hugged him.

"Ewww. You are sweaty. Get off of me," he said, trying to mimic me from earlier.

"You know you like it," I said.

"Yeah. I like it," he said. "You were a beast out there. Those women didn't know what hit them."

As we were talking, the coach walked over to us.

He smiled at me and said, "You were right. You were the best player on my team today. Good job Strong. I hope you'll be back next year."

A man in a blue suit was standing next to the coach and he said, "I hope we don't have to wait until next year for her to play again."

The man in the suit handed me a business card. I looked at it. The card had the name and logo for one of the city's women's basketball teams.

"I hope you can play in our basketball league. We would love to have you."

I told him I would think about it. Right now, I needed to go somewhere and sit down. The game had been fun, but I wasn't sure about doing that multiple times a week at practices and games.

I waved goodbye to my team members and then Toronto and I walked toward the park benches. We saw Officer Lifesaver and Officer Good Deed talking with a few other police officers near one of the picnic tables.

"Hey Strong, good game." Office Good Deed called out.

I nodded my head and gave her a smile. I guess she did recognize me.

We stopped to chat with the group for a while. As we were talking, I felt as if someone was watching me. When I turned around, I saw a man wearing a Police Department sweatshirt standing on the other side of the field staring at me. I got chills and turned back around really quickly.

Officer Lifesaver noticed and asked me if I was okay.

"Do you know who that guy is?" I asked him, gesturing to the man who had been watching me.

"I think he works at the Southside precinct. Why? Do you know him? Did he do something to you?"

"No, he didn't do anything to me. He just looks familiar and I have a bad feeling about him."

I didn't go any further. I didn't want to make accusations based on my strange feelings. I also didn't want Toronto to hear our conversation. He was very protective and would probably try to go over and confront the guy. Luckily, Toronto was talking to one of the other officers and didn't hear us.

After about ten more minutes of conversation, I told Toronto I was tired and ready to leave. We said our goodbyes and walked toward the parking lot. The man who had been watching me was now talking to a woman at one of the tables. I still could not clearly see his face, but I could hear him speak, and I couldn't help but think that I had heard that voice before.

***

The next morning as I was cooking breakfast, a breaking news story flashed on the television screen.

POLICE OFFICER FOUND DEAD AT LOCAL PARK

I turned the volume up to hear the full story.

"The body of a Southside police officer was found at Hyde Park early this morning after reports of fighting and loud arguments. The incident happened just after the annual FDPD Showdown. Witnesses say that the victim had been arguing with three men. According to one of the witnesses, one of the men accused the victim of sexually assaulting his sister. Investigations are still pending in this case, but you might remember this officer from a few years ago when he was accused of unwanted sexual advances by three local women. No arrests were made in those cases."

A picture of the dead police officer was put on the screen. I immediately recognized him. Not only was he the man from the park watching me yesterday. But I now also recognized him as the man who had groped me at the grocery store.

It's true - you reap what you sow. When you do bad things, bad things will happen to you. This man had assaulted lots of women. I knew that for sure. The three women who had come out against him in the past were only the tip of the iceberg. I thought about all the other women, including me, who never said anything. He had only groped me, but apparently there were others who had experienced a lot worse from him.

I thought about how Dr. Paradise had asked me if I reported him. My reason at the time was that I didn't think anyone would believe me. Now knowing that he was a police officer, I was certain that no one would have believed me. It would have been my word against his. But I wonder if I would have said something what would have happened. Maybe it would have been investigated. Maybe he would be looked at more carefully. Maybe even more women would have spoken up.

He certainly messed with the wrong woman this time.

CHAPTER 21
A Done Deal

· · · · · · · · · · · ·

"Hello, Strong. This is your attorney. Your former employer would like to offer a settlement in your case. Please give me a call so we can set up a time for the meeting."

The voicemail message surprised me. I had not heard from my attorney for months. I originally contacted her after I was terminated but she was always putting me off. Every time I called, she told me that no progress had been made on the case. I had totally forgotten about the case. I figured the lawyer had dropped the case since I didn't have any more money to pay her.

I returned the lawyer's call, and we scheduled a meeting time for the following week. The meeting was held at my lawyer's office and along with my lawyer and me, the company's lawyer and the Director of Human Resources were at the table.

"We want to express our sincerest apologies to you," the company's Human Resource Director began. "We have carefully reviewed your case and investigated the matter. We have determined that you should not have been terminated. You had stellar performance while you were with us and we want to bring you back to the company. We will give you back pay for all the time you have been away from the company and give you a bonus as well."

I could not believe what I was hearing. I was not at all expecting anything like this. At most, I thought they would tell me that I would get a small amount of money to quiet the matter. I would have never guessed that the company would apologize. And I definitely would have never guessed they would want to bring me back.

I let it all sink in.

"This all sounds good," I said. "But I am not sure if I want to go back to the office I was working at."

From talking to Premier, I knew that my termination had caused a lot of rumors. Not only had Edge told Golden that I tried to seduce him, but he told other people in the office as well. Even with me being vindicated, I knew that people would still be talking about me.

The Human Resources Director looked at me with understanding.

"What about moving to one of our other offices?" he asked.

I thought about it for a moment. "Maybe," I responded. "I liked the company a lot before I was terminated, and I really liked my job too."

The Human Resources Director told me that there were two Front Line Chief positions open at the other locations and I could choose one of those locations.

"Front Line Chief?" I asked.

That position would be a promotion from my previous position.

"Yes. With your experience and performance record, you would be a perfect fit. "

The company's attorney gave me some papers to review and as I looked over the documents, I saw that the back pay would be a substantial amount and that my new salary would be a huge raise.

I told them I would have to think about the offer. I wanted to take advantage of the opportunity, but I didn't know about moving to a different location.

When I got back home, I called Toronto and told him the news. He was very excited for me. I told him that I wanted to take the offer, but I wasn't sure about moving to a new city. The closest city was about two hours away. With Toronto and I being engaged, a big decision like this would affect our relationship.

"Every city has a fire department. I could relocate. Don't worry about that. I would be happy to move anywhere you go."

Tears flooded my eyes as I realized just how special Toronto was. I had never had someone who did so much to make me happy.

The next day, I called my attorney and told her that I would accept the offer. It took two weeks to finalize everything and my start date in the new position was set for the end of the month. Toronto applied for a transfer and we prepared for our move. In addition to the new job and back pay, the company covered our moving expenses and helped us find a new place to live.

After settling into our new home, Toronto and I could finally focus on planning our wedding. We decided to make it a simple affair and invite our closest family members and friends. During the negotiations and my conversations with the Human Resource Director, I found out that Mr. Energy had a big part in the company taking my case seriously and he was the one that insisted the company hire me back. I definitely had to invite him to the wedding.

Empower walked me down the aisle. We choose not to have bridesmaids and groomsmen, so it was just Toronto and me at the altar with the minister. As we said our vows, I was filled with so much love and joy. I felt like a fairy tale princess getting my happily ever after.

About the Author

· · · · · · · · · · · ·

Luxury Styles is from Seaside, California, overlooking the beautiful Monterey Bay. She took pleasure in writing and reading at an early age. Turning her passion into her priority was put on hold for several reasons. But now, she finally took it to another level and turned her ideas into a book. It's always been a Luxury to tell a story. What she thought was an uncertain dream is now reality.

To all those who have served and
those who continue to serve…

WE SALUTE YOU!

Thank you for your service and sacrifice!

CPSIA information can be obtained
at www.ICGtesting.com
Printed in the USA
LVHW042212230223
740254LV00009B/902

9 781950